The Hardest GOODBYES

The McLendon Family Saga – Book Five

By
D.L. Roan

Description

Some goodbyes are cathartic—a good riddance to those things that hold us back. Some are bitter-sweet. It hurts to say the words, but we know the pain is only temporary, and we'll soon be reunited.

Some goodbyes are *forever*. Those are the hardest to say.

At the height of the Cold War, Daniel and Cade's forbidden affair leads to a lifetime of love and loss, triumph and tragedy. Their ageless passion has forged an extraordinary family, and healed the hearts of those they love, but their journey was never easy.

From their first goodbye to their last, this is their story.

Never Miss A New Release

Direct from my insider's Writer's Cave Club, read exclusive excerpts, exciting character updates, behind the scenes editorials and more when you sign-up for my newsletter at www.dlroan.com

More Books by D.L. Roan

The McLendon Family Saga

The Heart of Falcon Ridge
A McLendon Christmas
Rock Star Cowboys
Rock Star Cowboys: The Honeymoon
The Hardest Goodbyes
Return to Falcon Ridge (Coming Soon)

Survivors' Justice Series

Surviving Redemption
One Defining Second

Blindfold Fantasy

First Print Edition 2016

ISBN-13: 978-1534741799

www.dlroan.com

Cover Design by JAB Designs
Copy Editing by Kathryn Lynn Davis
Proof Reading by Read by Rose

Interior eBook Design by D.L. Roan

Chapter One

The batter swung and, like a bullet, the ball flew over the pitcher's mound and soared towards the outfield. Daniel leaned forward in his seat, watching, hoping. The second baseman dove for the ball and missed. *Yes!* The ball landed in the sweet spot and bounced once before the center fielder picked it up and flung it towards home plate. *Run!* Collins pushed across the plate in a blur. Daniel pumped his fist in excitement.

"Out!" the announcer bellowed as the ref signaled the call.

"Bad call!" he shouted at the television screen. The slow motion replay was inconclusive and, much to his dismay, the call stood.

Damn Collins.

He looked at his watch. Ten more minutes before they needed to leave for Grassland's Fourth of July festival. He palmed the remote and turned the volume up a few notches to drown out the string of curses coming from upstairs.

"Dammit, I left them right here!" Cade's gruff voice grew louder. A door slammed—Daniel's cue to get up and help him look for his lost set of keys. If he didn't, Cade's ranting would get louder and he wouldn't be able to hear the game anyway.

He sighed and clicked off the television, giving up on his desire to see the final few pitches. The Mets were losing by three runs anyway. *Dammit all to hell.*

With a growl of protest, he pushed out of the chair and ambled into the kitchen, tossing the morning paper and checking all the usual places Cade could have left his truck keys.

"I don't see them down here," he shouted to his lover, who'd been tearing their upstairs bedroom apart for the last fifteen minutes looking for the damn things.

"Found them!" A few seconds later Cade stomped down the stairs, his irritation still evident in his expression. "They were in the bottom of the dirty clothes hamper again," he said with a sigh. "I can't remember shit these days. Must have left them in my pocket." He gave Daniel a peck on the cheek. "Thanks for helping me look for them, though."

"As if I had a choice," Daniel muttered under his breath.

"What?"

"Nothing. Ready to go?" he asked with a feigned smile. Pain in the ass or not, he still loved the man. He wished they shared a passion for baseball, but after more than a decade and a half of living with Cade, Daniel knew there was no hope of that ever happening. Cade was tough as nails, but he was a tech geek at heart, preferring to spend his time in his workshop turning everyday harmless gadgets into unassuming implements of destruction. Should they ever need it, their automatic vacuum cleaner could slice and dice an unsuspecting intruder's ankles to confetti. He'd admit it was an impressive machine, now that all the bugs had been worked out. Wearing armored socks had been a bitch.

"We're going to be late if we don't get going."

Cade opened his mouth to reply, and nothing but a groan came out. He tipped forward, his fist pressed to his sternum. His face twisted in pain and he blew out a labored huff.

"Are you okay?" Daniel guided him to the kitchen table and pulled out a chair.

Cade tried to brush him off, but sat anyway. "Just a cramp, or something I ate," he said. "It'll pass."

"When did this start?" Daniel picked up a glass from the rack beside the sink and filled it with water.

"Just now." Cade accepted the glass and took a sip, the pinched look on his face relaxing a bit.

Another good thing about living with someone for so long? You could tell when they were lying. "And the time before this?" Daniel persisted. "How long before it passed?"

Cade shot him a sideways glance, knowing he'd been made. The man may be a retired CIA spook, but he couldn't pull that shit on him and get away with it—not anymore. Daniel's years as a Federal

Marshal gave him his own internal bullshit meter and it was pegged into the red.

"It's nothing," Cade argued and stood. "Part of being an old fart, something you're as familiar with as I am." He slapped Daniel on the ass and downed the rest of the water before setting the glass in the sink. "I have to get a propane tank from the workshop before we leave. The regulator broke on the one Grey grabbed for the burger grill, and he's got a line of hungry kids at his tent, screaming for Cow Patty Sliders."

"I'll grab it," Daniel offered as Cade shoved his feet into his boots. *Old fart my ass.* "Meet you at the truck."

Shoving his concern aside, he left Cade to lock up the house and headed toward the old tack barn out back, which now served as Cade's mad scientist workshop. He opened the door and stepped inside, his aging eyes taking a moment to adjust to the darkness. When the room came into focus, all he could see was a tangle of half-naked limbs and torsos. The mass of flesh moved and Daniel froze.

It wasn't the sight of his grandson, Jonah McLendon, half-naked and tangled head to toe in the heat of passion that gave him pause. The kid was a horny teenager after all. Seeing *who* he was in a three-way lip-lock with, however, was like taking a line drive to the side of the head.

The girl was no surprise. Although Jonah hadn't officially announced their relationship to his family, Daniel and Cade had seen him with Chloe Jessop more than once, riding around town in his truck, doing whatever teenagers who think they're in love do.

He didn't know the girl, but her brothers were bad seeds. The oldest Jessop boy, Finn, had bullied his grandson from the time Jonah hit puberty until Finn graduated high school a year ago. Daniel suspected the only reason Finn's younger brothers hadn't continued Finn's legacy of abuse was because of Jonah's growth spurt. Over the summer he'd outgrown his dads—all three of them—by a solid foot and towered over the rest of the high school kids and teachers alike. He was a big boy, and he could take care of himself, but dating the Jessop girl would guarantee trouble. Toss in his best friend, Pryce Grunion, and the longstanding feud between the Grunions and the McLendons, and the kid was playing with fire.

3

"Shit!"

Jonah's whispered curse snapped Daniel out of his astonishment. "Excuse me," he mumbled and stepped backwards through the doorway.

"Papa Daniel, wait!" Jonah called out.

Daniel held the door open, his back turned to the room as Jonah untangled himself from the pile and righted what clothes he was still wearing before shuffling outside and closing the door behind him.

There were a thousand different questions and concerns running through Daniel's head, but he couldn't voice even one of them. Jonah was equally speechless, a contrite expression on his face, staring at the ground, the workshop, anywhere but at Daniel.

"Papa Da—"

"Is that the Jessop girl?" he asked at the same time.

Jonah swallowed whatever he was about to say and nodded silently.

"Are you and Pryce using protection?"

Jonah nodded again.

"Both of you? Even when it's just you and him?" Jonah's eyes widened and he shook his head, trying to deny what Daniel'd seen with his own eyes. "Remember who you're talking to, Jonah. You're not the first guy in the world to kiss another guy, and you won't be the last. Tell me you're being safe. That's all I care about."

"Yeah, we are," Jonah said and cleared his throat. "I know what that looked like, but—"

"What you do and who you do it with is nobody's business," Daniel said, holding up a staying hand. "You've told me everything I need to know."

Jonah gave him another nod, a deep flush coloring his face and neck.

He felt the kid's embarrassment all the way to his core. He'd tried to stifle his surprise enough to put Jonah at ease, but he couldn't stop the redness that crept up his own neck and filled his cheeks. Coming to terms with his sexuality as a grown adult had been hell on Earth. He couldn't imagine it was any easier for a seventeen-year-old kid. At least Jonah's family would love and support him.

"Do your mom and dads know?"

"God no! I mean—we're not—I haven't—"

"I won't say a word," Daniel assured him. "Just…" He cupped the back of the teenager's neck and gave it a squeeze. What should he say? The kid's dads had no doubt gone over the basics, but he was equally sure none of them knew anything about gay sex, or what might be going on inside Jonah's head.

"Sorry we crashed your workshop," Jonah offered, misunderstanding his reluctance. "It's kind of crazy at our place with Con and Car being back, and all the reporters and stuff. It won't happen again."

Daniel chuckled. *Sure it won't.* He did, however, understand the privacy issue. Jonah was one of five siblings in his polyandrous family. His older twin brothers, country music superstars Connor and Carson McLendon, had just returned home, cutting their latest concert tour short after the McLendon patriarch, Papa Joe, had a stroke. The reporters had been camped out in front of the ranch for days, trying to capture a soundbite or picture of the two, their camera drones hovering overhead at all hours.

Jonah and his twin sister, Dani, couldn't share an acre without bickering, and his younger brother, Cory—one year from getting his driver's license—followed Jonah around like a stray cat. Include Jonah's three dads—Matt, Mason and Grey McLendon—his mom Gabby, four grandfathers, including Daniel, Gram Hazel, and Uncle Cade, and Daniel wasn't surprised they'd been hard pressed to find a private moment.

"If you don't tell Uncle Cade, I won't," he offered. "But if that girl's father or brothers catch either one of you, I'm denying everything."

The first hint of relief ghosted across Jonah's face. His shoulders relaxed and a trace of a smile played on his lips. The kid knew damn well he was asking for trouble. *Like fathers like son.*

"Can you grab one of the spare propane tanks from the shelf in the back?" Daniel asked, letting the kid off the hook. "We're headed into town for the festival and your dads grabbed a dud for the hamburger station."

"What? Oh, yeah. Sure." Jonah bolted back inside like a spooked colt, returning seconds later with the spare tank. "Here ya go."

Daniel took the tank from Jonah's grasp, but stopped him before he could go back inside. "If you ever need to talk, about anything, I'm here. I hope you know that."

Jonah's chin dropped, his gaze fixed on the ground, his toes working into the plush green grass. "Thanks," he said.

When he offered nothing further, Daniel turned towards the house and made his way back to Cade's truck. Getting old felt like a curse most days, but he wouldn't give up a single day of his sixty-plus years if it meant going back to that place in his life. Even with the love and acceptance Cade and his family offered so freely, time had been the only thing to give him the confidence to accept who he was, and who he loved. Jonah would have to make those discoveries on his own. Daniel shook his head as he started the truck, honking the horn to hurry Cade along. He sure hoped the kid wouldn't make the same mistakes that had cost him so much precious time.

Two weeks later, Daniel stood in his grandson's hospital room, staring at his battered, sleeping form. A boy in a man's body, Jonah hadn't stood a chance against whoever had beaten the hell out of him. After what he'd witnessed in Cade's workshop, he had his suspicions, but any attempt at confirming them had been met by Jonah's fervent denial.

The poor kid had been found beaten and unconscious at the end of their driveway. With several broken ribs and a ruptured spleen, he'd been lucky his sister discovered him in time. The police found Pryce's truck alongside Jonah's at the rodeo arena where he'd been helping set up for an event, but Pryce's father Dirk Grunion, had insisted that neither he nor Pryce had anything to do with the attack on Jonah. Daniel hoped not. Jonah and Pryce were friends, and despite Dirk's adamant dislike of the McLendons, Daniel couldn't imagine him beating a teenager half to death. Chloe's brothers on the other hand...

"Did he tell you anything about what happened to him?"

Daniel turned at the sound of Jonah's mother's voice behind him. Gabby McLendon wasn't his daughter by birth, but he loved her as much as his own daughter, Natalie. Gabby was the reason he'd come to Falcon Ridge in the first place, the reason he and Cade had finally put their past behind them and fallen in love again. It was hard to believe so many years had passed since she'd married Cade's nephews and given him the grandchildren he thought he'd never have. He wished there was a way he could take her and Jonah's pain and make it his own.

"No," he said with a sigh as Gabby made her way to Jonah's bedside. "I…"

The urge to tell her about what he'd witnessed in Cade's workshop clawed at his resolve to honor Jonah's right to privacy. The boy would need someone he could trust, and Daniel wanted to be that person. Telling his mom about his sexual explorations wouldn't earn him that trust. But whoever had done this had damn near killed Jonah, something Daniel couldn't chalk up to boys being boys.

"You what?" Gabby asked when he didn't continue. "Do you know something?"

He shook his head and uncrossed his legs, resting his elbows on his knees. "I don't know what happened, but I'm sure we'll find out soon enough." He stood and pulled Gabby into his arms, hoping like hell he was right. "I should get home and check on Cade," he said, kissing the top of her head. "He's still hasn't recovered from the stomach bug he caught a couple weeks ago."

"Of course," she said with a shaky nod, brushing the wrinkles from the front of his shirt. A silly notion, considering he'd slept in the darn thing for almost two days. "Has he seen a doctor?"

Daniel gave her a dubious glare. "This is Cade we're talking about, remember? He'd rather get his arm caught in a sausage grinder."

Gabby's lips turned up into a tired smile. "Let me know if you need anything."

"I think you have your hands full already," he said with a weak laugh. "Call us if anything changes, okay?"

Gabby nodded. He gave her one last hug before he left, and not a moment too soon. Keeping secrets was Cade's specialty, not his. Keeping secrets from Gabby and the family, even for Jonah, went against every common sense instinct he possessed.

After spending two nights at the hospital, he was as wiped out as Cade had been the night before when he'd left to sleep off the stomach bug he'd been fighting. Daniel stumbled up the front steps and into the house. "Cade?" He tossed his keys on the kitchen table, taking note of the half-eaten bagel on the counter. *Stubborn man.*

He toed off his boots and hung his ball cap on the hook beside the door before going upstairs, unfastening the buttons on his shirt with each tired step. Cade stirred on the bed as he walked in, his eyes puffy with sleep.

"How's Jonah doing?" he asked, scrubbing a hand over his face before propping up on his elbow.

"He'll live," Daniel said with a sigh. "He's still not talking, though."

Cade grumbled and threw his legs over the side of the bed. "I'm going over to the Jessop place and have a word with—"

"You're not going anywhere until you tell me you've eaten more than half a bagel today." When Cade ignored him, Daniel's agitation level ratcheted up and boiled over into pissed-the-hell-off. "Get dressed," he ordered, bending down to retrieve Cade's pants from the floor. He balled them up and pitched them at him before searching their closet for two fresh shirts and a clean pair of jeans for himself.

"I thought you said we weren't going."

"I'm taking you to the hospital." Daniel's clipped tone invited no argument, but damn if the obstinate man didn't try to argue anyway. "This is *not* a negotiation," he warned. "You've picked at your food and hobbled around here for days, belly achin' about your belly ache. With Papa Joe's stroke and whatever the hell happened to Jonah, this family doesn't need more stress."

"Exactly," Cade argued, tossing his jeans aside. "I'm fine. I just got a little tired after all the commotion at the hospital."

"Because you haven't slept in a week!" Daniel picked up the jeans and threw them back at Cade. "Now put those on and get your old, stubborn ass in the truck!"

"Fine," Cade snapped. He shoved his legs into his jeans before he stood. "But I'm not going to the hospital. I'll go see Doc Pendercast."

"Doc Pendercast retired two years ago," Daniel said with a huff. "Dr. Hillsborough took over his practice and we don't have an appointment."

Cade snapped his fingers. "Is Margie Olson still the receptionist?"

Daniel shrugged. "I can call and find out, but we still don't have an appointment."

Cade snatched up his shirt and shoved his arms into the sleeves. "I'll call. Whoever's running that place now still owes me for the alarm system I installed. The least I can get is a damn appointment when I need one."

"That was five years ago. Let's just go to the—"

"I'm not going back to the damn hospital," Cade insisted and turned for the stairs. "I go in there and they'll pump me full of stuff I don't need. I'll end up worse than I am now."

Daniel followed him down the stairs. "Fine, but you're going if you can't get an appointment with Dr. Hillsborough."

An hour later Cade was stripped down to his boxers and sitting uncomfortably on the end of the exam table. "It's worse after I eat," he answered Dr. Hillsborough's question.

"Have you been running a fever of any kind?" the Dr. asked.

"No."

Daniel smirked at his curt reply.

"Lie back and let me take a look," the doctor instructed him.

Daniel cringed at the pinched look on Cade's face as the doctor pressed on his stomach.

"Does it hurt more when I press here, or here?"

"There!" Cade grunted. "Jesus, I could have told you that without all the poking around."

"Sorry," the doctor offered. "And how long ago did the symptoms begin?"

Daniel listened as Cade answered the doctor's questions, quite impressed that he didn't try to sugar coat his symptoms. A few more pokes and curses and the doctor helped him back into a sitting position.

"Well, it sounds like you might have a gallbladder infection, but I want to get a look at your pancreas, too, while we're at it, just to make sure. If it is a gallstone, it could be blocking your pancreatic ducts, which would be much more serious, but could explain some of the more acute pain."

"English, doc," Cade insisted with an impatient grunt. "What does that mean? What do I have to do?"

"It means you'll need to have a CT scan and some blood tests. Once I have a clearer picture of what's going on, we'll know better what we need to do next."

Cade glanced at Daniel, giving him a 'this *kid* is a doctor?' look. Daniel cleared his throat in warning.

"Fine," he groused. "Schedule me something for next week. That'll give me time to finish the new pantry shelves for my sister."

"Hazel will understand if you have to wait to finish them," Daniel said, resisting the urge to roll his eyes.

"Jake and Nate have already put it off long enough," Cade argued. "And Joe's been on their case since the freezer went on the fritz."

Daniel chuckled and shook his head in disbelief. Cade would do anything to get out of those tests, including handcuffing himself to said freezer. "Hazel's *three* husbands will do just fine without you for a day."

"I can't recommend you wait long," the doctor added. "If you have an infection or pancreatitis, it can be quite serious. I suggest you have the CT and bloodwork done today so we can get ahead of whatever is going on. If for nothing else, than to rule it out."

Cade closed his eyes and drew in a deep breath before he nodded.

"Great. I'll have Mrs. Olson call the hospital and schedule you into the first available appointment. You can drive straight over from here."

Cade's eyes narrowed to slits as he turned and scowled at Daniel. It took every ounce of willpower Daniel possessed not to say *I told you so*. He pressed his lips together to hold back his laugh. He was going to pay dearly for this, but he'd be damned if he'd regret it.

Chapter Two

Eighteen Months Later

Crisp, early sunlight streamed into the bedroom from between the gap in the curtains, the unfiltered beam illuminating the empty spot on the bed where Cade should be. It was Sunday. Sundays were meant for sleeping in. Daniel pushed himself up and swung his legs over the side of the bed, scrubbing his hands over his face to clear away the sleepy fog. Blinking against the sunlight, he glanced down at his aging hands and wondered when they'd become so wrinkled.

A muffled groan filtered through the quiet morning air. He turned his head to listen, unsure if it was no more than the grumble of his empty stomach. Another moan, this one louder and followed by a string of muffled curses, coaxed him from the comfort of the bed. He padded down the hall toward the bathroom, his old joints protesting his hurried pace.

"Cade?" The bathroom door was locked. "You alright?"

"Yes, dammit. I'll be out in a minute."

"Is it another attack?" He hated being a nag, but like his lover's stubbornness, Cade's gallstones weren't going away, and the pain was getting worse by the day. The last time this happened the doctor had recommended removing his gallbladder, but the doctor-phobic, headstrong man he was, Cade had opted to only have the gallstones removed, taking the chance they'd come back later. Apparently later was now and he could no longer afford to let Cade ignore them.

"You need to go see the doctor again."

The bathroom door swung open and Daniel took a step back. Dressed in his bathrobe, Cade leaned against the door, his brows pinched, his lips pressed together in a painful grimace, sweat glistening across his forehead. Dark shadows sagged beneath his hazel eyes as he huffed for each breath, his hand pressed to his sternum. "I'll call him tomorrow."

"You say that every time."

"Yeah, well, I mean it this time." He pushed past Daniel and grumped down the stairs.

Daniel snagged his robe from the hook on the bathroom door and followed him into the kitchen, making a beeline for the coffee maker. After pouring two cups and adding a teaspoon of cream to his lover's, Daniel reached over and grabbed his phone off the counter, setting both in front of Cade at the kitchen table. "Call him now."

"The coffee will help," Cade argued as he reached for the cup, ignoring the phone. "Besides, it's Sunday."

"So leave a message and you'll be at the top of the call-back list in the morning." Daniel watched as Cade's stubborn streak widened another inch. "Fine, I'll call." He snatched up the phone, flipping through his contacts until he found Dr. Hillsborough's number and dialed.

"Go ahead," Cade prompted, grimacing as the first taste of the strong, hot brew passed his lips.

Daniel waited for the recording to end and left a message requesting the first available appointment the next morning.

"Feel better?" Cade asked after he hung up.

"No,' Daniel said, taking his first sip of coffee. "I'll feel better when you feel better. You look like shit and it's getting worse."

"It's just another gallstone."

"Do you realize you've been fighting this since before Con and Car's wedding?" Daniel argued. Cade's grandnephews had married Joe's occupational therapist Breezy Youngblood, a year ago, and Cade's first procedure had been six months before that. Granted, he'd been fine for a year, but over the last few months he'd watch Cade fall right back into missing meals and sleepless nights, and now... He eyed Cade's physique with purpose. Yep, he was losing weight to boot.

"It's a simple procedure," Daniel continued, determined to make him see reason. "Laparoscopic surgery is as common as cheeseburgers now."

"Lapra-hooey," Cade said. "It's easy for you to say. You're not the one they want to cut open."

Daniel snorted. "Need I remind you of the six months I spent in a wheelchair after my spinal surgery?"

Cade's determined expression relaxed, his eyes softening as he remembered Daniel's return from India after taking a bullet that nearly shattered his spine. *Damn. How had twenty years gone by so fast?*

"I remember," he said, laying his hand atop Daniel's, giving it an affectionate squeeze.

Daniel laced their fingers together, noting the effects of time on Cade's hand. Twenty years didn't seem long at all. Something shifted inside him as the memories of their youth merged with reality. What if Cade was wrong? What if his pain was a symptom of something more serious? They hadn't had enough time. A lifetime wasn't enough.

"Daniel."

He looked up from their joined hands, some of his worry dissipating with Cade's reassuring expression. His quiet confidence had always soothed Daniel's anxious mind. Cade was like his personal control-alt-delete button, but this time there was something different, a look in Cade's eyes that Daniel had learned over years meant that he was holding back.

"I hate hospitals. You know that." Cade looked away. Pulling his hand free, he pushed to his feet and rounded the table. "I've let it go on too long is all." Daniel stood, and Cade pulled him into his arms. "I'll have the surgery and everything will be fine. Stop worrying about me."

"You like it when I worry about you," Daniel said and rested his forehead against Cade's.

"Not like that." Cade gripped the back of his neck in his steel grip. "Don't borrow trouble, old man."

"Old man?" he objected, giving Cade's shoulder a playful shove. "I may be an old dog, but I still know how to bury a bone." Daniel moved to pin him to the kitchen cabinets behind them, but stubbed his toe on the table leg. "Ow!"

He reached to brace himself on the chair, but Cade stumbled backward, his foot catching on the chair leg and dragging it from his reach. They flailed their arms, fighting for balance, until they caught each other, steadying themselves in time to stop from crashing to the hardwood floor in a tangled heap, and no doubt breaking a hip in the process. Breathless, his toe throbbing, Daniel clung to his friend and lover, who was laughing far too hard at his clumsy attempt at an early morning seduction.

"Like I said." Cade chuckled, giving Daniel's stomach a mocking pat. "Old man."

"I might be a little slow," he argued, "but I still know how to bring you to your knees."

"Wanna test out your theory in the shower?"

"Yeah." Daniel nodded, appreciating Cade's crooked, tempting smile. It may have been at his expense, but he'd exact his revenge in the best possible way.

"You think you can make it up the stairs, or should I call down to the ranch and ask Papa Joe if he still has that walker Breezy gave him after his stroke?"

"Fuck you," Daniel quipped, separating them with a friendly shove and hobbling on his injured foot towards the stairs.

"That's what I'm hoping for," Cade teased.

A knock at the front door stopped their retreat. "I'll get it," Daniel said, tying his robe closed with a loose knot and a wink. "Go start the hot water."

He watched as Cade climbed the steps, unable to miss the way he held his side as he walked. *Damn stubborn man.*

"Mornin', Papa Daniel!" His granddaughter, Dani McLendon, greeted him with a bright smile when he opened the door, a bundle of plastic grocery bags dangling from her arm as she breezed past him in a rush. "I know I'm early, but Mom slept in and the dads haven't gotten her out of the house yet. Since she doesn't know I'm coming, I thought I could hang out here with you and Uncle Cade until I can go over and start helping Breezy decorate."

"Decorate? Oh! The party is today?" He'd forgotten Gabby's birthday! "You drove from Billings this morning?" He shook his head as she emptied the contents of the bags onto the counter. Her

14

freshman year of college, she'd chosen to move onto campus instead of taking online classes, something her fathers had discouraged of course, which was probably the very reason she'd done it. Having three overprotective fathers could no doubt be a buzz-kill for a young girl just spreading her wings. Still, she shouldn't be on the road before dawn when she had alternatives. "It's barely daybreak. You should have stayed here last night."

"I wish I could have," Dani said with an exasperated huff, blowing a loose wisp of her long, dark hair from her face. "I have three back-to-back midterms next week and I needed to get in as much studying as I could, since I won't be back on campus until tomorrow night."

"You'll do just fine," he assured her. "You're a classic type-A McLendon overachiever. It's genetically impossible for you not to ace a test."

Dani paused, then reached out and wrapped her long arms around his neck. "Thank you, Papa. I needed that."

When she didn't let go, Daniel got an uneasy feeling in his gut. He took her in hand and held her away to look into her eyes. "Dani, what's wrong?"

She shook her head, a weak smile on her lips. "Nothing," she insisted. "I'm just stressed about school…and Jonah."

Daniel pulled out a chair for her and then took the seat across the kitchen table. Jonah never told anyone what had happened to him. Physically he'd recovered from his attack, but was still fighting an emotional battle no one fully understood. He'd left the ranch after high school graduation, telling the family he'd joined the Marines. It would have been an honorable choice, if it had been true. A few weeks after Jonah left, Cade—super spook that he was—decided to check in on the boy's progress at boot camp and discovered his ruse. After tracking him down and verifying that he was safe, Cade had decided it would be best to let a sleeping dog *lie,* in both senses of the word. Keeping their discovery a secret from the family was a decision Daniel struggled with daily, especially seeing the worry and sadness in Dani's eyes.

"He still hasn't called, huh?" Daniel asked.

"Nope." Slouched in her chair, all earlier traces of her excitement gone, she picked at the edge of the table with her glittery purple fingernails. "He hasn't called me in six months. I know we used to fight a lot, but he's never shut me out before—not like this. I don't understand what I did wrong."

"Oh, honey." He reached across the table and snagged her hand. "You didn't do anything wrong. Sometimes a man has to figure out who he isn't before he can know who he is. Don't take it personally, Dani. He just needs time."

Dani hesitated, but eventually nodded. It hurt his heart to see her so lost without her twin. He knew firsthand what Jonah was going through, and he wished there was a way to save the kid from it, but Dani shouldn't blame herself.

"He hasn't called Mom, either," Dani added. "With Cody moving out and starting his training at the Hastings Fire Department…" She blew out another exasperated breath. "Mom's losing it. The dads are hoping the surprise birthday party will cheer her up, but I can't help but think how weird it will be with everyone there except Jonah."

"Yeah." Daniel sighed and ran his hand over his balding head. "I can see where that might make his absence more acute."

Damn that boy. If only he knew how easy he had it. Compared to how the world worked back in his day, being gay nowadays should be a walk in the park. He and Cade weren't exactly the out-n-proud type, but he should have at least made the kid listen to him before he'd up and disappeared.

"To what do we owe this surprise?" Cade's booming voice filled the kitchen before he leaned down and gave Dani a peck on the cheek.

"Gabby's birthday party," Daniel reminded him, glad he wasn't the only one who'd forgotten. He'd never let Cade know that of course. "And you called me old. Maybe you should start some of those memory exercises we saw on that show we watched the other night."

"Oh! They have some awesome apps for that now," Dani said as she grabbed Cade's cellphone from the table, oblivious of Cade's extended middle finger behind her. Daniel gave him a sarcastic wink. "I'll download a few for you," she said. "I even use them sometimes to jumpstart my brain before I begin a study session."

"The only thing that needs jumpstarting around here is—"

"Have you eaten breakfast?" Daniel interrupted what he was sure to be a crude comment about their missed opportunity in the shower, something he wasn't about to discuss in front of his twenty-year-old granddaughter.

"I stopped for a breakfast sandwich on my way up, thanks, but I'll be glad to cook you guys an omelet if you want," she offered.

"No need," Daniel said as he pushed away from the table, giving Dani one last hug before he turned for the stairs. "It's your mom's birthday. He'll call," he assured her. "I'll go take a quick shower while you show your uncle some of those memory games. Then we'll head over to your parents' house together."

Chapter Three

"Shh! Here they come!" Cory, the youngest of the McLendon boys, said in an excited whisper. Daniel stepped into the study behind Cade as the family scrambled to hide. Cade's sister, Hazel, waited in the kitchen with her three husbands, Joe, Nate and Jake. Connor and Carson, Jonah's older twin brothers, raced to the top of the stairs with their wife, Breezy, to help her release the bag full of confetti they'd made. Cory dove behind the sofa in the living room and Dani stuffed herself behind one of the recliners.

The front door clicked open and Gabby sighed. "Thank you for a wonderful day," she said and turned to hug her husbands.

"It's not over yet, baby." With a wry grin, the oldest of Cade's nephews, Grey, pulled her into his arms and gave her a heart-warming kiss. Daniel watched through the gap in the almost-closed study door as Grey's brothers, Matt and Mason, took their turns kissing her. They weren't related by blood, but as the only true father Gabby had ever known, Daniel hadn't been too keen on the idea of her marrying three men. Looking at her now, and how happy Cade's nephews still made her, even decades later, made his chest ache with pride and joy.

"Surprise!"

The house erupted in cheers and song. Gabby turned and faced them all as they each made their way into the front room singing the most off-kilter version of Happy Birthday he'd ever heard. The only ones holding a tune were Con and Car, bellowing from the top of the stairs.

"Oh my God!" Gabby clasped one hand over her mouth, the other over her heart as she glanced among them all, her gaze settling on Dani. "You're home!" she squealed and ran to her daughter, wrapping her in an excited a hug. "I've missed you so much!"

"Mom, we talk on the phone and text almost every day."

Gabby shook her head and wiped away a stray tear. "It's not the same!"

"Happy birthday, Mom." Cory wrapped his strong arms around Gabby from behind and gave her a peck on the cheek. "Come see your cake!" He grabbed her by the hand and led her towards the kitchen.

"Happy birthday, Mom!" Connor, Carson and Breezy shouted before dumping the confetti over the railing, sending it spiraling through the air and landing on every available surface.

"Carson McLendon! I hope you're planning on picking that up!" Matt shouted up at his sons, but the look on Gabby's face when Mason picked her up and twirled her around under the shower of colorful paper, made every tiny scrap worth the effort.

Daniel snagged Gabby from Mason's arms and wrapped her in his own. "Happy Birthday, Gabriella. I love you, girl."

"I love you, too," she said, giving him a sweet kiss on the cheek. "And I can't believe you didn't tell me about this."

"Dani and Breezy threatened me with bodily harm."

"We did not!" Breezy said as she descended the stairs. "We might have said we'd name our first born sons after him if he didn't tell you."

"Who's having a son?" Grey appeared out of nowhere, his gaze laser focused on Dani. "Are you pregnant?"

"Oh my God, Dad! No!" Dani rolled her eyes. "It was a joke."

Grey's brows pinched together as he studied his daughter. Daniel choked back a laugh and Grey turned his scowl on him. "Not funny," he warned before marching off toward the kitchen.

"Oh, Breezy!" Gabby pushed from Breezy's arms, her expression charged with hope. "Are you saying you might be—"

"No." Breezy shook her head. "No babies yet." She held a finger to her lips and looked over her shoulder before continuing. "We're trying, though," she whispered.

"Oh my gosh!" Gabby bounced on her toes, pulling Breezy into another hug. "That's the best birthday news ever!"

"Shh," Breezy urged. "We haven't come to an agreement yet. Con and I are ready, but Car is still a little unsure."

"Oh, for goodness sake. What's he waiting for?"

Breezy giggled. "He's not exactly waiting. He just doesn't want to talk about it."

"T.M.I.," Cade interrupted, stepping over to give Gabby a gentle hug. "Happy birthday, darlin'," he said as he pulled Daniel towards the kitchen where everyone else had gathered.

An hour of McLendon birthday chaos later, after Gabby blew out the candles and opened the presents, Hazel cut the cake, which everyone devoured. Everyone except Cade. As the family sat around the dining table, sipping coffee and catching up on the daily grind of running the ranch, Daniel watched Cade pick at his untouched slice of cake. Cade had never been a fan of sweets, and it wouldn't have been a big deal, if he hadn't also skipped dinner.

"Con told me about the anti-drone system you set up for the ranch, Uncle Cade," Dani said, stealing Cade's attention from his plate. "Will you be able to program it to ignore the ones we'll be using to monitor the herds this winter?"

At the mention of the tech geek stuff he loved so much, Cade perked up. Daniel tried to listen as he, Dani and Matt discussed the modifications he'd have to make, but his attention was once again diverted when he noticed Gabby fanning herself with her napkin, another hot flash turning her neck and cheeks a fiery red.

Despite her enthusiasm about the surprise birthday party and Dani's unexpected visit, he could sense the melancholy she hid beneath her effortless, warm expressions. He also knew menopause wasn't the only source of the weariness in her eyes.

She caught his gaze and gave him a self-conscious smile. "They come and go at the oddest times. It's maddening."

He gave her a sympathetic grin. "Maybe Cade can invent an air conditioned shirt."

"I'd sell the ranch for one of those right now," she said with an exasperated sigh.

"It's just the beginning," Papa Joe, Hazel's oldest husband, warned her with a knowing grin of his own, his gaze darting to Grey. "I'm telling you." He shook his finger at Gabby. "You should go get some of those hormones before you—"

21

"Stop blabbering on about stuff you know nothin' about, Joe McLendon," Hazel cut in. "She'll do what she has to do when she's ready. Now stop badgering the poor woman."

"It's not her I'm worried about," Joe said with a grunt.

Daniel laughed out loud as Papa Joe sent Grey, Matt, and Mason a silent warning glare, mouthing the words *hide the knives* as he made a stabbing motion with his hand.

"I saw that," Hazel said, pointing at Joe.

The phone rang and Gabby jumped from her seat. "I'll get it. It might be Jonah."

Daniel tensed as he watched her hurry from the room. He hoped like hell it *was* Jonah. He wished the boy would stop the charade and come home. Lying to Gabby, to any of them, went against everything Daniel believed in, but Cade insisted they allow Jonah to make his own mistakes. It wasn't their place to interfere more than they already had.

"Oh, hi. Yes, it is my birthday. Thank you." Gabby's voice carried from the hallway.

He didn't need to see her expression to know it wasn't Jonah on the other end of the line. The disappointment in her voice was enough. He glanced over to Dani and found his own disappointment mirrored in her expression, too. Grey mumbled a curse which was echoed by Matt. Mason let out a long sigh and pulled his cellphone from his back pocket.

"I've left him two messages this week," Mason said.

"The last time he called, he said he'd be on a training exercise with no phone access," Matt reminded them.

"That was over a month ago," Grey grumbled, tossing his napkin onto his plate.

"Jonah's fine," Cade assured them. "If anything happened to him we'd have heard."

Heat flooded Daniel's chest and face. The ease with which the lie rolled from Cade's tongue made his stomach sour.

"I'm not worried something has happened to him," Mason said. "I think he's avoiding us altogether for some reason."

"He's sowing his wild oats," Cade argued. "Give him time. He knows where home is."

"I just hope it doesn't take him a decade to find his way back like two other ungrateful offspring we know," Matt said, glancing over at Connor and Carson, who shifted in their seats beneath the weight of their dad's glare. "Gabby's having a hard enough time as it is. A simple phone call on her birthday isn't too much to ask for."

The burning regret in the pit of Daniel's stomach continued through the evening and into the short drive home. Gabby's mood deteriorated after her conversation with Mrs. McEwin, and worsened as it became obvious Jonah wasn't going to call. Several times during the party he'd considered pulling Grey aside and telling him the truth, but his promise to Cade not to meddle kept him silent. They were a year into this lie, and telling the truth now would most certainly cause trouble, something he didn't want to do on Gabby's birthday. But he couldn't go on much longer, letting them believe Jonah's convoluted story.

"We have to tell them," Daniel spoke into the dark quiet of the truck cab as they pulled into the driveway, the glow of the porch light welcoming them home.

"We've already talked about this," Cade said with a sigh. "It's not our place to tell them."

"I can't keep lying."

"We didn't lie to them," Cade argued. "Jonah did."

"You're splitting hairs. Not telling them Jonah didn't join the Marines is the same as lying, and saying things like you did tonight only perpetuates that lie."

Why Jonah believed he could get away with such a farce in the first place was something he would never understand. Surely he knew Cade would verify his enlistment. Jonah broke Gabby's heart the day he left, and he couldn't stand by any longer and let her worry needlessly about her son's safety.

"Jonah needs time to come to terms with who he is," Cade said as he cut the motor and opened his door. When Daniel didn't move, Cade reached out and took his hand. "Just like you did."

"That's different, and you know it. I had a daughter to raise on my own, and when I lost her…"

"You had me to help you, and *you* know it, but you still chose to do things on your own, in your own time."

"And I wasted so much of that time," he argued. "What good is getting old if I can't use what I've learned to prevent my grandson from making the same mistakes?"

Cade grinned. "You know it doesn't work that way." He closed the truck door, encapsulating them inside the quiet darkness before he settled against the door. He was quiet for a moment, before he reached out and cupped Daniel's neck and drew him closer until their foreheads touched. "I hate seeing them worry, too," he said with sincerity, dulling the sharp edge of Daniel's resolve. "And contrary to what you might think, I don't enjoy keeping the truth from them either."

"I don't think you *enjoy* it."

"I don't," Cade insisted, his grip on Daniel intensifying with the conviction in his voice. "And as much as I hate to admit it, I think you're right. It's time Jonah stops running—but that doesn't mean we should be the ones to spill the truth to the family," he hurried to finish before Daniel could suggest doing just that. "We'll call him first. Let him know the jig is up and give him the chance to make it right first."

Daniel closed his eyes, releasing a guilt-laden breath. "I've already tried that," he said, shaking his head when Cade raised a brow. "He didn't answer or return my messages. I didn't say anything about knowing where he was." He admitted reluctantly, to himself at least, that he would have, if Jonah had returned his calls.

Cade released him and slouched back against the truck door with a sigh. "I hate flying."

"You're not going anywhere until you see the doctor," Daniel reminded him. "I'm not letting you wrangle your way out of that surgery again."

"We still don't know that I need surgery."

Daniel tucked his chin and gave him a dubious glare, shaking his head at Cade's willful denial. "I'll send Jonah an email tomorrow. If he doesn't respond, well, then I'll print it out and send it certified. If he ignores that, I'll either go get him myself, or tell Gabby and his dads."

Cade studied him for a moment, eventually nodding his agreement. "If it comes down to telling them, wait until I'm in surgery—*if* I have to have surgery. Maybe they won't give me so much shit for holding out on them if I'm all hobbled up in the hospital like an old mare headed for the glue factory."

"I don't think they use horses to make glue anymore," Daniel said with a wry grin. "Man, you really are getting old."

Cade raised his brow again, his crooked grin that had been Daniel's undoing so many years ago working its magic like it was only yesterday.

Germany - 1984

He could still smell the scent of fresh leather in the new Jeep he'd driven from the Embassy in Frankfurt, Germany to pick Cade up at the airport. When his commander sent him on the grunt's errand, he'd expected to meet another bloated, stuffy suit who would spend the entire ride back pretending Daniel didn't exist or, worse yet, some fresh-off-the-farm contractor who would pepper him with a million questions for which he had no answers. The singular upside of the assignment was that he was also picking up an old friend from high school, Garland Stolo, who'd managed to work his way up the ranks to Major and snagged a cushy attaché assignment at the Embassy.

Daniel backed the Jeep into the designated spot, cursing the snow that had coated the ground the day before, turning into a sheet of ice overnight and making every step a potential ass-buster.

Once inside the warm terminal, he stomped the snow from his boots and found his way to the gate. He checked his watch, confirming the ten minute wait until the flight was due. Satisfied with his timing, he surveyed the terminal for the best view of the gate and made his way up a dozen steps to an observation platform off the main thruway. His back to the wall, he crossed his arms over his chest and waited, taking advantage of the rare lull in his normally hectic schedule to just breathe.

Ten minutes passed too quickly. The plane landed and the door to the loading ramp opened. The first passengers began to file down the airstairs and make their way across the tarmac to the terminal. He

25

watched for Stolo, but the plane was too far away to identify faces. He pushed off the wall and made his way down to the bottom step so he could get a better look as a crowd of passengers from another flight filed by.

Stolo squeezed his broad shoulders through the doorway, throwing him a nod before he picked his way through the crowd to where Daniel waited.

"Major." He saluted his friend who returned the formal greeting before yanking him into a back-slapping, macho hug.

"Sergeant," Stolo said, his tone conveying his usual sarcasm in observation of their difference in rank, though they'd joined the military at the same time. "Still have no aspirations of grandeur, huh?"

"Nope," Daniel said with a chuckle, not a hint of disappointment in his reply. "Another year of shoveling brass-coated shit and I'll be at the top of the enlisted food chain. Beats being a pencil-pushing ass clown for the top brass any day."

Stolo's boisterous laugh bellowed through the terminal. "You never disappoint," he said as he grabbed his bag and turned to head out.

"Hold up a minute," Daniel said. "We're heavy one. Supposed to shuttle a suit to the annex."

"DIA? CIA? Alphabet Special?" Stolo asked.

Daniel shrugged as he glanced over his friend's shoulder. "Afraid that kind of information is above my pay grade, Major."

The line of people coming off the plane dwindled. He turned his focus to the doorway, looking for anyone who matched the dispatch report he'd been given. The last of the passengers filed by, and he was about to curse a blue streak when a lone male appeared at the opened plane door and ambled down the airstairs to the tarmac.

Cade Candelle walked through the gate, faded jeans and a leather jacket hanging from his lean frame, accentuating his slow, easy stride. Daniel's hand tightened on the stair rail as he watched the man move through the crowd towards him, the heels of his well-worn cowboy boots scuffing along the floor.

A chasm opened up beneath Daniel and something shifted—other than his dick. Locked in Cade's gaze, it seemed that everyone around them disappeared. Cade tilted his head, his lips drawing up into a crooked smile as lazy and carefree as the way he moved. Daniel's head swam with the impact of it all. This guy was no over-stuffed suit; that was for *damn* sure.

"You're not going to get shit from me, but if you don't roll your tongue back into your head, you're going to end up court-marshalled," Stolo said beside him.

"What?" The spell Cade had weaved around him broken, Daniel snapped his head up to see his friend staring down at him with an incredulous grin. "Shit."

He and Stolo were old friends, but they weren't *that* close. Nobody knew about his bisexual proclivities except for a handful of pseudonymous hookups he'd had throughout his life.

He'd learned that lesson the hard way his first month in boot camp when one of the guys in his squad decided he'd figured out his secret. After three weeks of cautious flirting, he thought he'd found someone he could trust and began flirting back. He'd genuinely liked the guy. They had a lot in common and their chemistry was off the charts, so when he'd asked Daniel to meet him down at the beach one night, he readily agreed.

Eight weeks of government sanctioned torture and a steady barrage of sexual advances he could no longer ignore, he was damn near to white-out conditions, and more than ready for his first real fuck since high school. What he got instead was the shit kicked out of him by the guy and his buddies in some obscure hazing ritual.

Luckily they'd kept their mouths shut and he made it through boot camp, surviving a constant barrage of vicious bullying before they all went their separate ways. As a result of his brutal initiation into the 'brotherhood', he'd become an island unto himself, navigating the precarious path between the truth and the lie he'd perfected.

He'd become so adept at hiding who he was, he'd earned the reputation of being the straightest guy in the Corps, which often put him in the crosshairs when the brass went on a witch hunt for homos, asking him to help ferret them out. He always denied knowing anything, of course, which led to its own level of speculation.

It went without saying that he avoided anything that invited further scrutiny, which was the driving force behind his reluctance to seek a promotion to a higher rank. Most days his secret was no big deal. His attraction to men came and went, depending on the man, so it wasn't something he felt the need to act on very often.

Whether it was because of his fear of discovery, or by design, he tended to lean toward women more than not, but the man in front of him blew whatever pie chart he'd stuffed himself into right out the window. The entire pie was filled with Cade Candelle—hot and gooey and bubbling over the edges with pure sex.

"Seriously, man. You're drooling," Stolo whispered and elbowed him in the side just in time to greet the cause of his salivation malfunction.

"What are you looking at?" Cade asked from across the dark truck cab, pulling Daniel from the vivid memory of the day they met.

He blinked the images away, pressing his lips together to hold back his telling smile. In days past, if Cade caught a glimpse of it, they'd have never made it inside. Tonight, however, they were no longer those two young lovers, and Cade needed to rest.

"Nothing," he said with a shake of his head. "I can't see shit in the dark."

"And you call me old."

Chapter Four

Memories of his past spurred Daniel from the comfort of their bed. Careful not to wake a finally sleeping Cade, he slipped on his housecoat and tiptoed from the room, down the stairs to the office they shared. He flipped open his laptop and logged into his email, clearing out his junk mail before he clicked on *compose new message.*

New Message

To: Jonah McLendon
Subject: The Jig Is Up

He grinned as he typed Cade's words in the subject line, but the serious nature of his email stole his smile. Unsure of how to begin, he let his fingers hover above the keys. What the hell was he supposed to say? He wanted to type out an order to return home and be done with it, but he knew Jonah. A blatant demand would merely strengthen his resolve. The McLendon stubborn streak ran strong and wide in his grandson, but he also had a sensitive heart. He was much like his dad, Mason, in that respect.

"Guilt it is," he whispered to himself and began to type.

New Message
To: Jonah McLendon
Subject: The Jig Is Up

Hello Jonah,

Papa Daniel, here, but I guess you already knew that. Wow, that sounds as awkward as I feel, but seeing as I've stared at the screen for ten minutes trying to figure out where to begin, I'm leaving it.

29

It's been a while since we've talked, so, I guess I'll get right to it. Today was your mom's birthday. Your dads took her shopping for the day while Dani and Breezy decorated the house for her surprise party. And what a surprise it was. Your mom cried, of course, when Dani and the rest of the family jumped out from behind the furniture to sing Happy Birthday. Connor and Carson dumped an entire trash bag of confetti over the stair rail, at which time your dads threatened hara-kari if they didn't stay to help clean up the mess.

It was a good day except, as we sat around the dinner table polishing off the cake your grandmother made, your mom battled back another hot flash. They're getting worse lately, and taking quite a toll on her, but I have to tell you, Jonah, the worst part for her, and Dani too, was not hearing from you. Her sadness and disappointment was profound.

Your uncle and I feel it's time to come clean, and that's why I'm writing you now. We know you didn't join the Marines. After you left, Cade got curious and did some snooping to find out how you were fairing in boot camp. Needless to say, it didn't take him long to figure things out. You can probably guess that it took him all of half a day to track you down.

How in hell you thought you could pull this off, with your uncle of all people, is beyond me. Jonah, I know you're smarter than that. I'm not judging your reasons for leaving, though I have a few things I'd like to say about that, too, but lying? To your entire family? Do you have any idea what kind of worry you've put them through? How hard it's been not to tell them?

He stopped typing and took a deep breath. Simply getting the words out lifted a huge weight from his shoulders, but the anger and frustration he'd harbored towards Jonah because of his actions became apparent as he read over what he'd typed. His finger hovered over the *delete* key. The last thing he wanted was to sound scolding and drive him farther away.

He read and re-read the few paragraphs again, deciding that, despite the reprimanding tone, the words needed to be said. Jonah needed to know that what he'd done affected more than just him.

I don't mean to scold you. Lord knows you have enough parents to fulfill that role. I may be your grandfather, but I'd thought, above all else, we were friends. The day I found you in Cade's workshop with Pryce and the Jessop girl, I meant what I said. You can talk to me about anything, without fear of judgment or shame.

You may not believe this, but I know more than a little about what you're going through. If you'll let me, I'm willing to share some of my mistakes and the steep price I paid for them. What I won't do is ignore the truth. Not any longer. So, I'm going to treat you like the man you want everyone to believe you are and call bullshit when I see it.

Even if you haven't figured everything out, you and I both know who you are. You're a good man, Jonah. You're better than this. Straight, gay or bi, there's nothing wrong with you. While I recognize your discomfort in sharing that part of yourself with an old man like me, the one thing I won't stand for is the shame I saw in your eyes when you left. Because you've chosen not to share what happened to you, I don't know what changed, but I know something did—obviously—to make you leave the way you did.

At the risk of sounding old—and don't you dare roll your eyes—I will say that, when I was your age, being gay didn't have a flag or face, and any monikers it did carry weren't friendly ones. I could barely admit to myself that I was attracted to men, and being equally attracted to women didn't help me figure things out any quicker. It was never a simple thing. Not to me. And especially not in the military. I know it's no simple thing for you either.

I'll admit, this is truly awkward to tell you, my grandson, but when I met Cade, my world changed. Everything I believed I was, what little bit of confidence I'd found in myself, was completely upended—turned inside out and shaken hard. While I was lost in my attraction to him, at the same time, it scared the hell out of me.

Daniel leaned back in his chair and closed his tired eyes, inviting his memories to take him back to the day he met Cade. The day that changed his life forever.

Germany - 1984

31

"You my ride to the annex?" Cade asked, tilting his head towards the terminal exit.

Daniel was frozen in place, an internal instinct warning him that, lurking behind those deep green eyes, was a world of secrets and mystery. Cade was no bloated suit, and when he winked at Daniel, he knew the bastard was well aware of the effect he was having.

"Yeah—eh-hem—right this way." Forgetting Stolo was beside him, Daniel turned and plowed into the Major. "Fuck, sorry." He shook himself, ignoring the heat that bloomed beneath his shirt collar.

The frigid air outside hit his fevered skin like a cold shower, washing the lust-infused fog from his brain, but not in time for him to remember the ice-covered parking lot. His foot flew out from beneath him and the sudden loss of balance sent him careening into Cade.

"Whoa, Boss." Cade laughed as he wrapped his arm around Daniel and helped him regain his footing. "I think you're sexy and all that, but we just met."

Stolo laughed out loud and slapped Daniel's back. "We're Marines. We have two speeds. Fast and hard."

"Sorry." Daniel pushed away from Cade, giving Stolo a silent middle finger. He managed to keep his feet beneath him long enough to get everyone's bags loaded. When he opened the driver's door, he hesitated, expecting Stolo to take shotgun. No such luck. Cade slid into the front seat and propped his boot on the dash.

"Do you mind?" he asked, nodding at the dash and the wet snow dripping from his boot. "It's new."

Daniel didn't know why the thoughtless move irked him so acutely. It wasn't his job to clean the Jeep. Maybe it was a way to take back a little of the control the man had so effortlessly stolen from him. Maybe he was just being a prick. He didn't know or care. All he wanted was to get the fuck out of whatever alternate universe Cade had sucked him into and get his charges to their assigned destinations. And then get skunk-ass drunk.

"No problem, Boss," Cade said with a slow drawl and another knowing grin as he lowered his foot to the floorboard. Daniel watched him work his pant leg up, pull a sheathed knife from his carryon and drop it down into his boot. "Was feeling a little naked without René."

"René?" Daniel managed after, yes, imagining Cade naked. What the hell was so damn different about him? Some men were more attractive than others, same as women, but he'd never before had such a visceral reaction to either. "You named your knife René?"

"Kind of sexy, don't you think? Vanadium steel." He drew the knife from its sheath, holding it up for Daniel to admire. "Hard and rigid, yet silky smooth."

Daniel swallowed against the knot in his throat as he watched Cade run his finger along the edge, a line of crimson appearing along the paper-thin cut when he reached the tip. "And it will slice you open with so little effort, you'll bleed out before you even realize you've been cut."

Daniel blinked, his gaze snapping from the blade to Cade, and then forward as he started the Jeep. *Okay. Not gay. Message received loud and clear.*

He spent most of the ride back in silence, listening to Cade and Stolo trade home brewery secrets. Apparently, in his youth, Cade had specialized in bootlegging moonshine in Tennessee, something Daniel didn't find odd at all for some strange reason. Cade had that country rebel, backwoods way about him.

They pulled up to the annex and the large wooden gate swung open, quickly closing behind them when Daniel drove through, sealing them off from any onlookers or passersby's inquisitive gazes. He'd driven by the place a dozen times since he'd taken the assignment at the Embassy, but never seen inside the compound walls. He'd probably never know for sure, but if he had to guess, he'd say it was an outpost or an analyst shack for a CIA op.

Fearing his gaze would travel to places it shouldn't, he stared straight ahead in silence as Cade stepped out of the Jeep and shouldered his bag. Stolo got out and made his way around to the front. "Nice to meet you, Major," Cade said and shook Stolo's hand.

"Same here, man."

Daniel thought he was in the clear when Stolo slid into the front seat. He was about to pull away when Cade ducked down and peered back through the open window.

"Thanks for the ride." he said, giving a mock salute. Daniel chanced a glance at him just in time to catch another of his flirty winks. "I owe you a beer."

Daniel snapped his gaze back to the windshield and gave a careless wave. "We're good. No problem." *Asshole.*

He cursed his shaky voice before shifting the Jeep into gear, and left him standing in the middle of the annex's courtyard. Whatever the hell kind of head games the spook was playing, Daniel wasn't about to be the dumb fucker who fell for them, no matter how attractive he was. Not again.

The day couldn't have ended fast enough. Once cleared by security at the Embassy, he and Stolo went their separate ways, promising to meet up later for beers. As much as he loved the selection the local German breweries offered, he needed something stronger to dispel the lingering thoughts of one Cade Candelle.

After a hot shower and shoveling down a plateful of something he couldn't pronounce at the Embassy cantina, he was ready for a shot with a little fire to it. Five shots later he received a message that Stolo wasn't going to make it. Five more shots later and he stumbled into his bed, face down, clothes on, pictures of Cade's easy, smiling eyes mingling with the darkness.

"Hey." Cade's gravelly voice jolted Daniel awake. He looked up to see a black screen on his laptop, the morning sun reflecting his old, sleepy face back at him. "Were you down here all night?"

"Shit." He scrubbed a hand over his eyes and two-day-old beard. "I guess I dozed off while I was writing to Jonah."

"Must be a real page turner," Cade joked.

"It is." Or at least his memories were. He turned and looked Cade over, taking in his crisp clothes, freshly shaven jaw and the energetic look in his eyes. "Looks like someone slept well last night."

Cade stretched his arms over his head. "I did. I feel like a million bucks today. Haven't even made coffee yet."

Daniel narrowed his eyes. "You're still going to the doctor today."

Cade stretched his neck from side to side before he rolled his shoulders and let out a sigh. "Yes, I'm still going." He dropped his arms and strode over to Daniel, running his palm over his prickly hair. "I guess after twenty years, I'm never going to get you to grow your hair out, am I?"

He'd kept the high-and-tight military buzz, or some variation of it, over the years. He didn't think his barber knew how to cut another style, even if he'd asked him to. "What are the chances you'll watch the World Series with me?" Cade's silence was exactly the answer he expected. "Besides," Daniel continued, running his own hand over his balding scalp, "not much left to grow."

"Good point," Cade said on the heels of a yawn.

"Did the doctor's office call you back?" Daniel asked, ignoring the friendly jab. He pushed to his feet, his knees and back crackling like a damn popcorn machine from spending the night in the desk chair.

"Yes," Cade said with a scowl. "They can get me in at nine-thirty."

Daniel peered down at his watch, holding his arm out until the hands came into focus to show the late morning hour. "Better make that coffee while I go take a shower, then. We're not missing this appointment."

"You don't have to go with me, you know," Cade said as Daniel followed him from the office to the foot of the stairs.

Daniel kept walking, taking each step with care as he made his way to the top. "I haven't fallen for that trick in more years than I can count. Now, go make me some coffee."

Chapter Five

Thirty hours later, Cade sat on the sofa, the words on the pages of the book in his hands blurring in and out of focus. The longer he looked at them the less sense they made. Having forgotten the premise of the story, he closed the cover and let the book fall to his lap, adding it to the already enormous pile of pointless and failed distractions he'd tried to employ.

After a full panel of bloodwork, enough x-rays to turn him into a mutant anti-hero in one of the comic books he'd collected over the years, and a cupful of chalky dye he was ordered by Nurse Ratchet to drink, he was told to go home and wait for a call from the doctor.

The longer he waited, the more convinced he became that his body was fighting more than just a simple gallbladder infection. He didn't know what, but something was different this time. He could feel it, and if he was right, the thought of seeing the unexpected grief in Daniel's eyes made him even sicker to his stomach than he already was.

The sound of Daniel's fingers tapping the keyboard traveled through the office doorway into the living room where Cade sat. He looked up to see him hunched over his laptop, typing out another email to Jonah, no doubt. He'd hoped Jonah would reply to the first one, but the hacker buddy he'd asked to ping Jonah's email had written back to say he hadn't opened it yet. Considering the spotty signal where he was, Cade doubted he'd even received it. He hoped for Daniel's sake that he did soon. If all the *ifs* they were running from ever caught up to them, Daniel would need the family, all of them.

He watched as Daniel typed, unable to stop the grin that pulled at his lips as his lover hunted and pecked each key, his tongue poking out the corner of his mouth with the effort. All of the *'old man'* jokes aside, the years had been kind to them both. Wrinkles and all, he could still see the tall, broad-chested soldier he'd fallen in love with, ghosting through the much older man he loved infinitely greater than he'd imagined possible in those early days.

Daniel had enthralled him from the very beginning. Cade had never met a man he could so easily read. From the moment he laid eyes on him, he knew their story would be one of those gripping sort of tales he'd never want to end. He also knew it *would* end, causing nothing more than heartache for them both, if he stuck around long enough to read it through.

Frankfurt, Germany – 1984
Three Days Later

At the pinnacle of the Cold War, Germany was Cade's break-out assignment. He'd worked his way through a slush pile of cases until he got his hands on one that had the potential to make him a major player on the international stage. If he succeeded at completing his assignment, he'd be in no position to pursue a relationship with anyone, romantic or otherwise. He could never be one of those agents who lived a double life, with a wife and kids who thought he worked at a printer repair company, or some equally ridiculous cover. Not that he'd ever wanted a wife or kids. His family was big enough without him contributing to the chaos. Being gay was irrelevant. His path was set, and he would not deviate from it.

Why then was he standing in front of the annex Chief, insisting he request Sergeant Gregory to replace their defunct driver who was laid up in the hospital, mourning the loss of his appendix.

"Embassy personnel aren't an option," the Chief said with a stern shake of his head.

"You didn't have a problem using them as a shuttle service to pick me up from the airport. Don't tell me you can't issue another request," Cade argued.

"We'll postpone."

"We can't postpone," he insisted. "I've worked this case from the beginning. Ackerman isn't stupid. The second we get shifty he'll disappear and we'll miss our window." Careful not to let the chief see how much this case meant to him, he schooled his expression and shoved his hands into his pockets, giving the man a careless shrug. "It's no big deal. If you can't secure Sergeant Gregory to fill the position, we'll nix the op and I'll go back home. I'm sure Langley will understand, considering what a clusterfuck the regional logistics have been, with talk of the wall coming down and all."

"You don't honestly believe that propaganda bullshit, do you?" The chief peeled his glasses from his face and threw them onto his desk. "Hell, Candelle, we've been seeding that intel for a decade. That wall isn't going anywhere anytime soon."

"Maybe you're right." Cade folded his arms over his chest and gave another casual shrug. "But if it does, we're going to need the names on that list."

"Why Sergeant Gregory?" the Chief asked, pinning him with what he thought was an intimidating stare.

This was a question he was prepared for. Why he'd spent the last three days combing through every piece of intel he could gather on the Sergeant was something he didn't want to examine too closely, but what he'd found gave him the perfect excuse to request his services for the job. His personal interests were of no consequence.

"He's spent time on the defensive line in Fulda Gap. The roads up there are a snarled nest of sheep trails. He'll know them if we need to use them, and I trust him."

"You just met him three days ago!"

"I just met *you* three days ago."

While his sarcasm was evidently lost on the Chief, his reasoning was spot on. Six hours later Daniel was standing in the Chief's office, dressed in his fatigues and trying desperately not to look Cade in the eye.

"Lose the uniform," Cade ordered, holding back his grin as Daniel's gaze darted upwards, his eyes widening in surprise.

"Here?" Daniel choked out, nervously fingering the top button of his shirt. "Now?"

"No," Cade said with a chuckle, taking note of the way Daniel's chest fell with his silent sigh of relief. "I'm assuming they instructed you to bring a change of clothes."

"Yes." Daniel lifted his bag from the floor.

"Good." He grinned and nodded at the bag. "The more casual the better. If all things go as planned, you'll just be taking an unexpected tour of the countryside. But in this world, Murphy's Law still rules and we don't want to attract the wrong kind of attention if we have to deviate from the plan."

"What plan is that again...exactly?"

Cade opened the office door and motioned for Daniel to follow him. "I'll deal you in once you're in your civvies and we're on the road." He led him through the cluttered analysts' hub and down the hallway to the restroom. "You can change in there, then meet me in the room at the end of the hall. And hurry up. I need to brief my team about the change in plans."

"Wait," Daniel said when he turned to leave.

"Do you need help?" Cade asked, giving him a playful wink. He was fucking with the poor bastard; even though it was cruel, he couldn't seem to help himself. But a part of him, a very insistent and neglected part, hoped Daniel would accept his sarcastic invitation, fist his hands in his shirt and yank him into the bathroom with him. A dozen hard-on inducing images flashed through his mind before Daniel's brows furrowed and he shook his head.

"No. I'll be right out."

As the bathroom door closed, Cade released a breath he hadn't realized he'd been holding and leaned against the doorframe. Why in hell was he torturing himself like this? It wasn't as if they'd have any time or opportunity to fuck on the hour and a half drive to Hünfeld.

Resigned, and confounded by his inability to shut the man out of his head, he turned and walked down the hall, shaking off the absurd desire to wait by the door.

Once on the road, he relaxed into the passenger seat and propped his boot on the dash. Daniel gave him a sideways glance, but didn't offer his earlier rebuke. He grinned and lowered his foot anyway.

"It's not my car, man," Daniel scoffed with a wave of his hand. "Do whatever makes you comfortable."

That was not an invitation. Cade bit his lip as he repeated the mantra silently to himself. "How long have you been in Germany?" he asked, though he already knew the answer.

"Two years, give or take," Daniel said as he flipped on his signal and made the turn onto the highway, watching in the rearview mirror as the other vehicle in their two-car convoy fell in behind them with ease. "Are they going to be following so close the whole way?"

Cade looked out the back window and grimaced. "Wanna lose them?"

"What?" Daniel snapped as he glanced between Cade and the rearview mirror. "I thought they were part of your team."

Cade glanced over his seat once more at the other car, considering his options. He didn't need or want a four-man team for this op, but going into a highly fluid situation without eyes in the back of his head wasn't smart.

"Look," Daniel said with a huff, "I'm not supposed to be here. I was asked—ordered—to drive you to Hünfeld and back, not to go on some—"

"I was joking." Cade held up his hands. "It was a joke." He straightened in his seat and propped his foot back on the dash. Prompted by a need to feel his hard flesh beneath his palm, he reached over and squeezed Daniel's thigh. "You need to loosen up, Boss."

Daniel slammed on the brakes. Tires screeched along the pavement and Cade braced himself against the dashboard until the car slid to a stop on the side of the road, their tail car almost crashing into them.

"I haven't asked the first question about what the hell is going on or why I'm here," Daniel said with a commanding tone Cade couldn't help but find sexy. "Not that I expect to get anything close to a straight answer from you, so I'm not going to bother asking. But let's get one thing straight. I'm Embassy security, not some spook tool you and your CIA buddies can order around like a trained dog. I take my orders from my commanding officer, and those orders did not include putting up with your bullshit."

His tirade all but over, Daniel turned away and stared through the windshield, his fingers drumming nervously on the steering wheel. "I get it, okay? You're not...into me—that...whatever. You made yourself perfectly clear the other day, but don't think for a second that I can't, or *won't*, put you on your ass the next time you touch me. Stop the fucking head games and keep your hands to yourself."

Cade studied Daniel, his surprise laced with lust. Soldier Boy had teeth, and balls. He liked balls…a lot. That he struggled to say the word 'homo' was telling, and stoked his curiosity. Had Daniel ever fucked a man? Had he ever been fucked? All questions he'd get answered one way or another before this trip was over. Finding out what made Daniel Gregory tick had just become his secondary mission.

"I was wrong," he admitted with a shrug. "You don't need to loosen up a little. You need a complete stickectomy."

"Fuck you," Daniel muttered and pulled the car back onto the road.

Soon, my new friend, he thought with welcome anticipation. *Very, very soon.*

The next half hour passed in uncomfortable silence. Cade used the time to watch without watching. Every detail intrigued him—the way Daniel breathed; the way he tugged on his earlobe when he had something to say, but was debating whether or not to say it. And then the way he'd shift in his seat when finally deciding not to say it, as if keeping the words bottled up made him physically uncomfortable.

When Daniel reached inside his pocket and pulled out a pack of gum, Cade watched his fingers as he unwrapped a piece and folded it into his mouth, taking note of his neatly trimmed fingernails. They were a stark contrast to the thick calluses on his palms.

"Want a piece?"

Cade reached out and took a stick from the pack, sliding the peace offering into his shirt pocket to save for later.

Daniel eyed him at the odd move, but said nothing as he tucked the pack back into his coat pocket.

"Trying to quit smoking?" Cade asked to keep the crack in the proverbial door that had opened between them.

"Na," Daniel said, chewing the fresh piece of gum. "I quit a while back. Now I'm working on my alcohol problem."

"How the hell does chewing gum help you with that?" he asked with a genuine laugh.

Daniel shrugged again, running a hand over his dark blond, high-and-tight military buzz. "It makes me want a cigarette instead of a drink."

Cade shook his head. "Nice circle jerk you got going there."

"It works, until it doesn't."

"What happens when it doesn't?"

Cade grinned at Daniel's failed attempt not to laugh, his lips parting into a heart-stopping bashful smile, dimples and all. "I get drunk and wake up feeling like I swallowed an ashtray."

"And then you start over?"

Daniel nodded.

"How long since you last quit?"

"Drinking or smoking?" Daniel asked as he navigated around a slow-moving box truck in the lane beside them.

"Both. Either."

Daniel scrubbed a hand over his freshly shaven jaw. Cade wondered if he was calculating the days, or deciding whether or not to lie.

"Three days ago," he finally said, a crimson hue creeping up his neckline to flood the tips of his ears.

Warmth bloomed in the pit of Cade's stomach. He didn't know whether to feel flattered or ashamed. He couldn't remember a time when he'd had such an extreme effect on someone without a month's worth of planning and design. He also knew that made him an asshole. He'd taken advantage of every opportunity to use Daniel's obvious attraction for a little fun, but the jig was up. It was time to come clean before Soldier Boy cut him off completely.

He pulled the strip of gum from his pocket. The scent of peppermint mixed with the frigid air teased his nose before he folded the stick into his mouth, wondering if he would still be able to taste the strong flavor on Daniel's tongue when they kissed for the first time.

"I was only fucking with you earlier," he admitted, shoving the thought away until later, when he could act on it.

Daniel furrowed his brows in confusion, but kept his eyes on the road. "So you said."

"No. I mean, before that." Christ, he really had been a prick. He shifted in his seat. He wasn't accustomed to apologizing, but he wasn't above it, either. He just didn't know how to say it without sounding like a lust-struck sucker.

"Forget it," Daniel said. "I mean…we're cool."

"You misunderstand me," he said.

"I got it," Daniel rushed to assure him. "Let's talk about something else."

Cade swallowed his confession, nearly choking on the words, but decided to let it go. Maybe taking the long way around would work better. "Okay, what do you want to talk about?"

"I don't know," Daniel said, his jaw ticking as he chewed his gum. The man had more nervous tells than a broke poker player down to his last stack of chips. "You said you ran moonshine. Ever get caught?"

He had to think a minute before his conversation with the Major came back to him. "Oh, that! That was all bullshit," he said with a chuckle.

"What was all bullshit? You didn't run moonshine?"

"Nope. Not a drop. Never even tasted the stuff."

"Then, why did you...?" Cade cringed beneath the weight of Daniel's glare as the truth hit him like a brick between the eyes. "You were playing Major Stolo?"

"It was too easy not to!" he said with an apologetic grin. "The accent, the back woods lilt to his words."

"Jesus! You're one scary dude." Daniel shook his head in disbelief. "Why would you do that?"

Now it was his turn to shrug. "Lying is ninety percent of what I do. I guess it's hard to turn it off sometimes. Besides, the good ol' boy network is huge, and you never know when you might need to pull a Major's name out of your ass."

"So you're not from Tennessee, then."

"Illinois." He schooled his expression as Daniel turned and studied him.

"Lie," Daniel finally said and turned his attention back to the road.

Cade laughed. "You're getting better at this."

"Seriously. It's a simple question. Where are you from?"

He hesitated, but figured it couldn't hurt to give him a little of the truth. "Montana. I grew up in a small town a few dozen miles north of Billings."

Daniel eyed him again before letting out a frustrated sigh.

"What? It's the truth," Cade insisted.

"Whatever you say, man. I'll never know the difference."

"Fine." Cade shifted against the door to face Daniel, using his body language to communicate his willingness to give an honest response. "Ask me another question, anything you want, and I'll tell you the absolute truth."

Daniel glanced skeptically between him and the road a few times. Would he take the bait? *Come on. Ask me. Are you gay?* Three little words and they could stop dancing around the subject and heat things up a few notches.

"Are you an only child?"

The air rushed from Cade's lungs in a disappointed huff. *Shit.*

"Seriously? You get a free pass and that's the one question you want to ask?" Did he have to spell it out for him?

The corner of Daniel's lips ticked up into a sly smile. "Hey, you said any question."

Was he being intentionally obtuse? Who was fucking with whom, here? *No, it's not possible.* The guy's attraction to him was debilitating. As oppressive as the military must be for men like him, there wasn't a chance in hell he'd pass this up if he thought for one second they played for the same team. Disappointment fused with frustration and he sighed again. Soldier Boy was a tough nut to crack.

"I have a younger sister," he admitted. "She's married to three men, so technically I have three brothers, too."

"Bullshit!" Daniel spat.

"Swear to God," he said, crossing his finger over his heart. "Even I couldn't make that shit up."

"Seriously?" Daniel asked in disbelief. "She's married to three men?"

"Three brothers to be exact," he confirmed. "They have three kids, too. All boys."

Daniel's confused expression looked almost painful. "H-how does that work?"

Cade shrugged. "Beats the hell out of me, but it does. She seems happy, at least."

"That's fucked up." Daniel cupped the back of his neck as he tried to imagine the scenario, something Cade tried not to do too often. "They have balls, I'll give them that."

"Tell me about it," Cade said. "It makes being a homo look like a walk in the park."

Chapter Six

"Shit!" Daniel cut the wheel and darted over to the right lane just in time to make the off ramp. Angry drivers blew their horns and swerved out of his way. He glanced in the rearview to see their tail car didn't make it, watching out his side window as it rolled past them in the far lane, the driver indicating they'd make a U-turn.

"I'll pull off to the side a ways down and wait for them," he said, pissed he'd let himself get distracted by more of Cade's head games.

"Or you could keep going and we can grab a pint of beer while we wait."

"Do they know where we're going?"

"There's only one town along this road before we get to Hünfeld, right?" Cade asked.

"Yeah, but—"

Cade waved him on. "They're big boys. They'll figure it out."

Daniel bit back his argument and continued down the narrow two-lane road, everything inside him rioting against the idea. As a Marine, he was trained to never leave a teammate behind, but it seemed the alphabet leagues played by a different set of rules, if any rules at all.

Neither the winter scenery nor the sound of the road beneath the tires were distracting enough to keep his thoughts from wandering back to the infuriating man beside him.

For one split second he'd thought he had the upper hand. Cade was baiting him and he wasn't biting. The second he asked him if he was gay would be the second he reached for that shiny knife he kept in his boot and spouted off another veiled threat. He'd seen his share of that shit—guys who got their rocks off making those in the closet sleep with one eye open every night. He'd grown more adept at hiding his sexual preferences since that night on the beach, until *him*.

Well, he wouldn't be losing any more sleep over Cade Candelle either. He didn't give a damn if his sister was married to an entire herd of jack-a-lopes. The man didn't know shit about what it was like to be anything other than a straight-up hetero asshole.

Cade pointed to the first pub that came into view. Daniel navigated the slush-filled potholes to the empty side street and parked. The warm air inside the dark pub hit him like a suffocating wet blanket and he peeled off his jacket.

"Order one for me, will ya?" Cade said before he walked to the payphone on the back wall.

Daniel tossed a few Deutschmarks on the bar and held up two fingers, nodding when the barkeep said he'd bring the round to the table. He took a seat by the window and watched for the other car. He was halfway through his pint of Löwenbräu when he found himself staring at Cade instead.

Cade caught him gawking and smiled.

He jerked his gaze away, focusing on his glass before he tipped it back and chugged what was left. Fuck quitting. If he hadn't already lost his mind, he would before this trip was over, and drinking would be the least of his problems.

Cade hung up the phone.

His head down, his gaze fixed on the tabletop, he listened to the sounds of Cade's boots scuffing along the floor in his signature lazy gait. Why did he find that so sexy?

"I thought you quit." Cade nodded to the glass cradled in Daniel's palm.

"And here I thought you were being an insensitive prick." Daniel raised his empty glass and toasted Cade's full one. "Here's to being *just* a prick."

"Listen." Cade sighed as he dropped into the chair across from him. "I know you think I'm full of shit—and in all fairness, I am most of the time—but—"

"You could have given us a warning before you went all Evil Knievel out there!"

Falk, the taller of the two other spooks, stormed through the front door. Once again distracted, Daniel hadn't noticed the tail car pull up to the curb out front. Falk tapped on the inside of the window and motioned for the driver to park and come inside. "Fucking hell, man." Falk stomped over to their table and hovered beside Daniel. "If that's the best you can do to keep a tail, what the hell are you even doing here?"

"Funny," Daniel said, his tone dripping with sarcasm. "I'm still wondering the same myself."

"Sit the fuck down," Cade ordered Falk. "He's here because I need him." He kicked the chair beside him out from under the table and pushed his untouched beer in front of him. "Take a load off and have a drink."

Falk shrugged off his coat and sank down into the chair with a mumbled curse. Daniel pushed back from the table, the sound of the chair scraping against the floor echoing through the otherwise quiet pub. He didn't need this shit.

"Going to take a leak. Feel free to leave without me."

As soon as the bathroom door swung closed, he braced himself against the small sink and sucked in a series of steadying breaths. If he thought the laid back, sexy, who-gives-a-fuck Cade was irresistible, seeing his playful green eyes turn to steel, accompanied by the restrained power in his voice when he spoke to Falk, was like adding gasoline to an inferno.

I need him.

Those words undid him. Before he could get a grip on his imagination, all of the graphic visions that flashed through his head, and his body's involuntary response to them, the bathroom door swung open.

Cade stepped inside, staring at him through the mirror's reflection. Daniel's heart rate skyrocketed. His lungs demanded more air than he could seem to find in the suddenly too-small restroom.

"Get out," he ordered. He couldn't do this. Not here, not now. This thing he had for Cade couldn't be contained in such a small space, and if the man so much as cracked the first joke, made even a single backhanded comment, or—so help him God—touched him, there would be no turning back. He'd walk back to Frankfurt if he had to.

"Hey, Boss. What's—"

"I said get out!" He jerked away from Cade's outstretched hand, but Cade grabbed his sleeve and wouldn't let go.

"It's okay," Cade said in a soothing tone, but it wasn't okay. Didn't he get it? Didn't he see that being in the same space, in the same goddamn country with the homophobic asshole, had driven him mad within a three day span?

Cade's lips turned up into that fucking crooked smile that made Daniel want to push him to the floor and bury himself balls deep inside him. Of course he knew. The bastard was mocking him, pushing him beyond his limits and making him look like a fool.

"Go to hell!" Daniel growled and shoved him away, but Cade held on, gripping him tighter.

Daniel freed his arm and took a swing. Cade ducked and grabbed him around the waist, shoving him into the wall with more force than he'd expected from the leaner man.

He fisted his hands into Cade's shirt and shoved back. Their struggle upended the small trashcan in the corner, snarling their feet and legs and throwing Daniel off balance. He fell into Cade, who spun them around until he was once again pinned from hips to shoulders against another wall.

Heat swamped his body and ran like lava through his veins as he stared down at Cade. As predictable as the sun, his dick reacted to the closeness. He tried to move away, but with the cold tile at his back and Cade's hot, hard body pressed against his front, he was trapped. If Cade had any questions about how much he wanted him, the insta-boner pressed against his hip answered every single damn one of them.

The room fell silent except for their labored breaths mingling together in the inch of space between their mouths. The temptation to look down at Cade's lips was overwhelming, but he held his gaze, refusing to give him the satisfaction. Daniel wanted more than anything to give up and give Cade what he'd been asking for, but the second he did, he'd be nothing but a joke to him.

When Cade looked away first, and lowered his gaze to Daniel's lips, his heart stuttered. He teetered on a tightwire between hope and all-out war. Was Cade going to kiss him, or was he about to have to kill the fucker?

Cade reached up and cupped his hand around Daniel's neck, drawing him down until their lips nearly touched. Air rushed in and out of Daniel's flared nostrils as he struggled to breathe. His shoulders shook with adrenaline as every fantasy he'd had in the last three days manifested in front of him. Was it possible? Was this real?

Cade closed the distance between them, crushing their lips together. Daniel forgot to breathe as he opened his mouth, their tongues meeting in a long, all-pervading stroke. Then another, and another. The heat, the need, the longing he'd felt for so damn long, but rarely gave credence, all came together in a tight ball inside his chest, and then exploded.

He clutched Cade to him, eager for more. Cade tilted his head and gave it to him freely, releasing an impatient growl of his own as they struggled against one another to get closer, feel more, taste deeper. It wasn't enough.

As if he'd read Daniel's thoughts, Cade gripped his ass and hauled him closer, grinding their cocks together in time with each deep stroke of his tongue. The last breath Daniel took rushed out through his nose and he sucked in another lungful of air, then another, the fresh supply of oxygen and the feel of Cade's hands on him going straight to his head. He felt himself falling, sinking to the floor, but Cade held him pinned against the wall, kissing him until his shock faded and the only feeling that existed was the rightness of it all.

"Peppermint and beer," Cade finally said in a breathless whisper against his lips. "Not my favorite, but when you mix in the hot soldier it has a nice bite."

Forehead to forehead, Daniel couldn't look up at him. He still didn't trust this—whatever *this* was—and if it wasn't real, he didn't want to see the ugly truth in Cade's eyes. He wanted to hold onto his fantasy a moment longer, but Cade cupped his hands against his cheeks and forced his head up. When Daniel lifted his gaze, he wanted to believe the mirrored hunger he saw was sincere, and not just a reflection of his own desires.

"We have to go." Cade pressed his lips to his one final time, nipping his bottom lip before he pulled away. "Are you still with me?"

Unable to speak, Daniel nodded. At least he thought he was, if his legs worked better than his tongue.

Cade released him and then straightened his shirt. "We'll talk about this later, okay?"

Daniel nodded again, reluctant to let him go as Cade backed away and opened the door, disappearing as it closed behind him once again. *What the hell just happened?*

Numb and on auto pilot, he flipped the lever on the faucet and splashed some cold water on his face before he followed Cade to the car, surprised he remembered to snag his jacket from his chair on the way out.

Twenty minutes later he blew past the small inn they were looking for. He wasn't in any condition to be driving. He didn't remember a single mile that had passed beneath the tires since they left the pub—not a road sign or vehicle. That kiss filled every crevice of his mind so vividly, everything else had faded to static in the background.

He mumbled a curse as he looked for a place to turn the car around. Cade snickered beside him. Daniel looked over to see him propped against the door, resting his head on his fist as he stared out the windshield, smiling like a Cheshire cat that had just found a new mouse to toy with.

That look scared the shit out of Daniel. Was it possible Cade was as blown away by what'd happened as he was, or was he playing him? *Did he only kiss me because he needed me to stay?* He'd never met a man so calculating and purposefully confounding, but he'd also never experienced a kiss so intense. No matter what kind of head games he might be playing, nobody kissed like that unless they meant it. *That kiss was real. Wasn't it? Fuck.*

"Pull over here," Cade instructed after they waited for a battery of armored tanks to pass.

Falk and his partner were parked across the street from the inn, eying him with comedic disdain as he rolled past them and pulled into the empty parking lane in front. He gripped the steering wheel a little tighter in an effort to keep his middle finger in check. If anyone needed a stickectomy, it was Falk.

"Stay here." Cade got out of the car and jogged up the steps into the inn, coming back a few minutes later. "Park around back and go up to the room," he instructed as he handed something through the open window.

Daniel stared at the object dangling from Cade's finger. A key. To a room. No one said he'd be staying the night. Somewhere between ecstatic and about to vomit, he peered up at Cade, swallowing against the sudden dryness in his throat before he glanced back at the key.

"Go on. Take it." Cade shoved the key into his sweaty palm. "I'll be up in a bit."

Daniel watched as Cade walked around the car, crossed the street and handed a similar key to Falk. *Go!* Cade motioned for him to move. Daniel blinked away the images running through his head and shifted the car into gear. Move. Park. Room. *Fuck.*

Were they going to fuck? What were they going to do in that room? He knew what he wanted to do, but holy shit. Was he really going to fuck Cade Candelle? What if Cade wanted to fuck him? His ass clenched in response to the thought. He'd never let anyone fuck him before. Was he going to let Cade?

This was moving too fast. He wanted...whatever the hell Cade wanted, but...shit! He'd thought...he didn't know what the hell he thought anymore. He hooked the wheel and turned into the last empty space behind the inn, misjudging it by a mile and almost rear-ending a station wagon. He didn't even know how to park!

His hand trembled as he slid the key into the lock and turned it, thankful he didn't break the damn thing off. Once inside the room, he dropped his overnight bag on the floor, ran straight to the bathroom and flipped open the tap. The ice-cold water stung his face and hands, leaching into the cuffs of his long shirt sleeves. He didn't care. He needed a jolt, something to snap him out of his near hysteria so he didn't explode in his pants the second Cade walked through the door.

Through the mirror, he eyed the shower stall behind him. Water that cold would do the trick, but did he have time? Cade said he'd be up in a bit. What the hell was a *bit?*

"To hell with it." He was acting like the fool he'd thought Cade was trying to make him out to be. Maybe he still was. Well screw that. It wasn't as if he'd never fucked a guy before. It had just been a while since that particular itch had been scratched. A long while.

He snatched the cheap hand towel from the rack on the back of the door and scrubbed it over his face and head, picking a piece of lint from his hair before he flipped off the water and walked into the bedroom.

The matchbox-sized room was dim with a single full-sized bed and an antique night stand. A small writing desk sat against the opposite wall, its sole adornment a telephone. A few minutes from sundown, the stale air was downright frigid, too. He switched on the single lamp in the corner and searched out a heating source, unable to find a vent or thermostat.

Hünfeld was nothing more than an eighteenth-century farming village in the middle of the most probable Soviet rout of attack if they decided to invade the West. With its half-timber structure and shake roof, the inn was no doubt as old as the town, and by the looks of it, the owners hadn't bothered with upgrades since before the Second World War

The door opened and in walked Cade, carrying several black satchels and a silver hard-shell briefcase. Daniel's heartbeat quickened and the temperature inside the room shot up ten degrees. Who needed a heater when you had Cade Candelle?

"Help me with these?" Cade held a duffle bag out to him, dropping the hard case and another backpack onto the floor.

"Yeah, sure." Daniel shook off his edgy reaction to Cade's proximity, gathered the bags from his hands and lined them up on the bed as Cade turned and locked the door behind him.

"Here." Cade picked up the backpack and handed it to him. "There's a bag of pens and markers inside. Get them out, dump them on the desk and unplug the phone.

He did as he was told, half looking through the bag, half watching Cade as he retrieved several old maps of Germany from one of the bags and pinned them to the wall behind the desk. Bag in hand, he reached in and scooped out the pens, setting them in a neat pile on the desk.

"No, like this." Cade reached over and shuffled the pens so they were scattered about the desk in a messy arrangement. "We want it to look random."

Daniel shrugged and unplugged the phone from the receptacle, wondering what in the hell Cade was doing and why he seemed in such a hurry. When Cade took out a fat, felt-tip marker with a tiny black lens in the end, and clamped the attached wire to the phone line before he plugged it back in, it didn't take long to put two and two together.

"Holy shit! You're a spy!"

"Shh!" Cade shouldered him out of the way and unscrewed the cap on the phone's handset. "I'm counter intelligence. My job is to catch the spies."

Daniel took another step back, his pulse racing faster than he'd like to admit. "You're here to catch a Soviet spy?"

Cade declined to answer his question, giving him an incredulous glance that made him feel like an idiot for asking. Of course he wouldn't tell him that. "How do you know *I'm* not a spy?"

Cade whipped around and drilled him with that damn hypnotic gaze of his, sending Daniel's blood racing to all the right places. "Are you a spy?" he asked, his warm breath caressing his chin.

Daniel swallowed, hard, his eyes drawn to Cade's parted lips. "No."

"That was easy," Cade said and turned back to whatever he was doing with the phone.

Speechless, and more than a little intrigued, Daniel watched as he fingered the bug into place and screwed the cap back onto the receiver. He suddenly felt like he was in a spy novel, and didn't know if that was a good or bad thing.

"Um, should I…should I be here? I mean… I'm not going to see something you'll have to kill me for later, am I?"

"No." Cade laughed as he worked. "It's only a meeting. When I get confirmation that my contact is on their way up, you can go into the room next door with Falk. I'm sure the two of you can find something to talk about without killing each other."

Daniel snorted. "I doubt that. What's his problem with me anyway?"

"Jealous, I suppose," Cade said. "He's been trying to suck my dick for the last three days."

"Falk?" What the… "Falk is gay?"

Three loud, angry knocks rattled the wall from the room next door.

"Roger that," Cade said. "All set in here."

Daniel slapped his hand over his gaping mouth. "He can hear us?" he whispered through his fingers.

Cade nodded and brought a finger to his lips. He grabbed Daniel's hand and tugged him into the bathroom, where he closed the door, flipped on the shower and crushed his lips against Daniel's in another devouring kiss.

Chapter Seven

Daniel scrambled for purchase, clutching at Cade's shirt, his arms, the doorframe—anything he could get his hands on to keep his balance as Cade shoved him against the closed door and went to work on his belt. Gripped by staggering lust, a shudder raced down his spine, and he tensed beneath Cade's touch. He reached for Cade's jeans, his fingers moving with frantic purpose to work the button loose.

"Christ," he panted against Cade's neck, sucking in a shaky breath when Cade reached inside Daniel's pants and wrapped his fingers around his dick with a commanding grip. His coordination shot to hell, Daniel's hands fell to his sides as he melted against the door. He hadn't felt a man's touch in so long he'd almost forgotten the difference.

"We have fifteen minutes, twenty tops," Cade said as he sank to his knees. "Now *this*. This *is* a surprise," he said, and licked him from root to tip before he swallowed him whole.

"Jesus!" Daniel threw his head back against the door so hard, he wasn't sure if the stars he saw were from the blow to the back of his head, or from Cade's hot mouth sucking the life out of him.

Cade released him. The cold air kissed his wet foreskin, sending a shiver along his spine.

"You're getting awful preachy up there," Cade said with a devious grin, his hand gripping Daniel's shaft with exactly the right pressure. "Didn't figure you for a religious man. Not with a dick like this."

He looked down at Cade, watching with awe as he pushed back his foreskin and tongued the underside of his cockhead. *Holy fuck!* He was going to come. He wanted to come, needed to come, but he squeezed his eyes closed, forcing back the orgasm barreling toward him like a runaway freight train. He couldn't. Not yet. Not so soon.

When Cade closed his lips around him again, his knees buckled. Daniel braced himself against the door, his breath rushing in and out through his gritted teeth. What was this man doing to him? It was too much. Not enough. He was losing his mind.

Desperate for equal footing, Daniel shoved his hands into Cade's loose curls and pushed him off his cock. Cade glanced up, the look in his eyes a mixture of lust and confusion. Daniel wrenched him to his feet and kissed him, the newness of Cade's unique flavor exploding over his tongue as he backed him against the sink.

His fingers no more steady than they had been the last time he'd tried, Daniel worked Cade's button loose and pushed his jeans over his hips. Cade's lips turned up into a grin against his own when he palmed Cade's dick and found it every bit the size of his own, circumcised and hard as steel. "Don't worry," Cade whispered against his lips. "I have no religious objections to whatever you want to do with me."

The promise in his voice, the way he said the words... Daniel sucked in another fervent breath. As many times as he'd imagined being with Cade, he was a million miles away from knowing what to do with him now that he had him.

Cade pushed up to sit on the edge of the sink, putting them at the same height and aligning their cocks in his hand. A chasm opened up beneath him when Cade wrapped his hand over Daniel's and began to stroke them together. Cade's cock against his, their hands moving in tandem, was unlike anything he'd ever felt. Daniel bucked beneath Cade's touch, pressing himself farther into the space between his open thighs.

"That's it," Cade said, reaching around with a free hand to grab Daniel's bare ass and pull him even closer, pressing them together from balls to tip. "Oh yeah."

Steam billowed from the shower and swirled around and between them, making the air thick and heavy and hard to breathe. Daniel closed his eyes and lost himself in Cade's kiss until the rhythm they'd set caught up to them. A chorus of muted sighs and groans filled the small space, adding another sensual layer to their union, which grew louder with each stroke.

The first euphoric spasm gripped Daniel's balls and he grunted a string of curses through his clenched teeth. He couldn't hold this one back, nor did he want to. He gripped Cade's thigh with bruising strength as his orgasm was ripped from his body, stroke after vigorous stroke.

Cade seized the back of his neck, forcing him closer, his mouth opening over Daniel's to capture his moan. The kiss was deep and long and zealous, pulling him onto his toes as his body tensed and then released what felt like his soul, his cum spilling over their joined hands.

Cade squeezed his thighs tighter around Daniel, his hips bucking up with abandon, over and over as he came, his hot seed mixing with Daniel's.

Forehead to forehead, he melted against Cade. Neither of them made any effort to move, except for their chests heaving with their attempts to catch their breath.

"Damn, I needed that," Cade whispered against his cheek, his thumb caressing affectionate circles on the back of his hand.

Cade's tone brought Daniel back to the moment, reminding him there was nothing more to what they'd done than two guys who were attracted to each other, letting off some steam. He hoped like hell he got more than this one chance, but hearing the truth in Cade's voice made him realize that he'd hoped for more.

Hope was a dangerous thing when it came to wanting more, because there couldn't be any more than this. Not with Cade. Not with any man. Even if society were more accepting, his military career would be over if anyone discovered his secret. Lying might be Cade's specialty, but it wasn't his. Hiding who he was, day to day, was difficult enough. Doing so around Cade had already proved impossible.

"Yeah." Daniel sighed and lifted his head, putting some much needed space between them. "I needed that, too."

Any reply Cade may have had was killed by the shrill sound of the telephone ringing.

"Shit! I have to get that." Cade pushed him away and jumped down from the countertop, rapidly washing his hands in the sink before he buttoned his pants and sprinted into the bedroom to answer the call.

Daniel braced against the sink and stared at his reflection, the cold air from the bedroom rushing in and corroding the fog on the mirror. His eyelids were still heavy with lust and pleasure, his skin pale and clammy with sweat and steam. He looked tired.

With one last resigned breath, he admitted he *was* tired: tired of hiding who he was, tired of second guessing every move with Cade. Even after what they'd just done, a part of him still wondered if this was real, if Cade was only using him. He'd read spy novels. He knew some agents were trained to have sex with whomever they needed, gay or straight, if it suited their mission.

He closed his eyes and let the last ten minutes settle inside him, his cock responding to the remembered feel of Cade's mouth. So what if he was using him? He needed this, dammit, and wanted more. He'd let Cade take what he wanted for however long this lasted, and soak up everything he could before he returned to whatever reality awaited him back at the Embassy.

Their one-day trip turned into two after Cade's meeting was postponed and they were forced to drive to Hamburg. Those two days led to an affair he could only look back on as euphoric.

Over the next few weeks, every free second of their time was spent driving the countryside, or sitting on the rooftop of Cade's ramshackle apartment building, sharing a joint and a case of German beer, until they were both frozen, shit-faced and laughing so hard Daniel felt like he'd done a thousand sit-ups the next day. When they weren't sitting around with a buzz, talking about home, or debating which comic book characters had the ultimate superpower, they were making out on the flimsy mattress in the middle of Cade's bedroom floor.

"I can't believe you don't at least have a bed," Daniel said, staring at the large water spot on the ceiling as he savored what remained of his high. Cade's place was nothing more than a room in a converted motel that was long-since past its prime. Peeling paint, outdated wiring, scuffed and buckled wood floors were highlighted by the stark lack of furniture or personal effects that would indicate anything but rodents lived there.

"Like I said," Cade sighed from his prone position beside him, "I won't be here that long."

Cade *had* said, and Daniel didn't need the reminder. They hadn't talked about where this was going, or wasn't, but he had a feeling when Cade left, he wouldn't be back.

The weeks they'd been together were the best of Daniel's life. He'd tried to keep himself in check, not getting emotionally attached, but the thought of returning to his solitary life B.C.—*before Cade*—was more than depressing.

"When do you think you'll be reassigned?" He loathed the needy tone in his voice. He shouldn't have asked, but the more time he spent with Cade, the more he feared he'd drive over one night after work and find nothing but an empty room, all traces of their time together vanished.

Cade rolled over and threw his leg over him, snuggling close beneath the blanket as he nuzzled his lips against his neck.

"We still have time," he whispered into his ear, flipping the tip of his tongue along the outer shell, inducing a shiver that made them both groan.

It was a lie. He was no better at reading Cade than he'd been the day they met, but Cade had shared more than was assuredly appropriate about what he did for the government. They both knew he could be pulled out of Germany at a moment's notice.

While he hadn't calibrated his bullshit meter to *Cade Candelle specs,* their time together had proven Cade could be trusted with his secrets. He'd told Cade about what happened to him that night on the beach and why he was so guarded when they first met. After swearing a blue streak, Cade laughed about the mixed signals, admitting that his need for a driver was nothing more than a contrived effort to spend more time with him.

During one of their nights on the rooftop, Daniel also confided that he'd never let a man fuck him. When he'd finally puked up the confession, he hadn't expected Cade's reaction, or lack thereof. While Cade offered to *rectify* his anal virgin status, posthaste, he hadn't pushed for anything more than the hand and blow-jobs Daniel was more than willing to give, even introducing him to a few other creative pleasures, but it wasn't enough.

He wanted Cade, craved him. If there was ever a time to take that step, or a man with whom to take it, it was now, with Cade, before he disappeared and he lost his chance.

"I want you to fuck me," he whispered against Cade's neck before he lost his nerve. "But you have to use a condom." The AIDS stuff was scary shit. Nobody could seem to agree on what did or didn't cause it. He'd heard horrifying tales of the fatal disease, and the military was testing for it continually. Aside from not wanting to die miserably, he was already pushing his luck. Popping a positive on a dope test would be bad enough.

Cade stilled against him, the feel of his cock hardening against his hip in immediate response. He pushed up on his elbows and hovered above Daniel before he reached over to the side of the mattress and grabbed a tube of lube and a condom.

"Aren't you going to—"

"Shh." Cade placed his finger over his lips as he settled himself between Daniel's parted thighs. "I know what I'm doing." He grinned. "I've wanted to do this from the moment I saw you." He paused and glanced up at Daniel. There was an honest openness in his eyes Daniel had never seen before, giving him confidence he'd made the right choice. "I'll make it good for you. I promise."

Daniel swallowed whatever concerns he had, nodding his silent consent.

Cade hooked his arms beneath Daniel's knees, lifting and parting his legs, shoving both pillows under his ass. Daniel held his gaze as Cade kissed his left knee, his inner thigh, drawing out a groan of approval when he reached his sac and tongued his way along his shaft, then back down again.

"Told you I'd make it good for you," he said with a promising wink.

"Just do it," Daniel ordered, his insides already shaking with the powerful mixture of need and trepidation.

"Oh no," Cade said with a chuckle. "I said I'd make this good, and that's exactly what I intend to do."

"Wouldn't this be easier if I rolled over onto my—holy fuck!"

He gripped the blanket beneath him with both hands as Cade slid his tongue from his balls down to his asshole.

"Relax," Cade instructed, using his forearm to press his hips back down onto the pillows.

"Fat chance of that," Daniel said, followed by a mumbled curse as Cade spread his legs wider apart and continued where he'd left off.

Daniel closed his eyes and tried to force himself to relax, focusing on Cade's hands as they roamed his body. His lover's kneading fingertips worked their way over his hips, caressed his sides, and teased his nipples into taught peaks, all while he circled the rim of his ass with his tongue, until suddenly everything he was doing wasn't enough. Daniel reached down and gripped his cock, stroking himself once before Cade stopped and sat up between his knees.

At the loss of Cade's touch, he opened his eyes and looked down to see him applying the lube to his fingers. He took a deep breath and relaxed. This he could handle. This he was ready for.

Several times over the last few weeks he'd let Cade explore, growing accustomed to the odd sensation of his finger inside him, and even coming to crave—*son of a bitch!* "Damn!" He wasn't prepared for the second finger. Less prepared for the third. The burn was intense, but he breathed through it, forcing the air from his lungs through his nose until the sting faded, morphing into an intense need for more. Daniel was torn between begging or reaching down, taking Cade by his hips and forcing him to fuck him.

"You should see the look on your face," Cade said as he cupped Daniel's knee with his free hand, pushing his leg up until he was spread wide for whatever Cade wanted to do. "I can't wait to get inside you."

"So don't wait," he gritted out, bearing down on his hand. The whole room spun as Cade's finger passed over his prostate. "Holy—sonofa—fuck, do that again! That's…fuck." Like nothing he'd ever felt before. Cade was turning him inside out! When Cade stopped and pulled his fingers free, he didn't know whether he wanted to come, or curl up into a ball and cry.

"Remember to relax," Cade said.

Breathless, he watched as Cade rolled on a condom and applied a generous amount of lube. The sight of him stroking his shaft had Daniel licking his lips. He'd become intimately familiar with Cade's cock over the last few weeks. He'd touched and tasted every inch of it, and the thought of every one of those inches inside his ass made him shudder with both fear and anticipation.

Cade braced himself on one outstretched arm, hovering above him as he positioned the tip of his cock with his other. Daniel sucked in a breath when he felt the tip kiss his rim.

"Open your eyes." Cade gripped his chin and forced him to look at him. When their gazes met, Cade rolled his hips and the tip of his cock slipped inside.

"*Ffffuuuck.*"

Cade stilled, his grip on Daniel's chin tightening. "Look at me," he insisted. "The hard part's over."

Daniel opened his eyes, not even aware he'd closed them again. Cade smiled down at him, his calculating gaze conveying something he was sure he didn't want to examine too closely, lest he lose more than his ass to this man.

Cade began to move, pulling out and pressing in a little further with each stroke. Daniel held his gaze, breathing through the pain until his body relaxed and all he felt was full.

"That's it," Cade whispered against his lips. "Feel me."

"I can't feel anything *but* you," he panted.

"Good." Cade pulled out and pushed back in. "I don't want you to ever forget the feeling," *slow slide out,* "of me inside you," *slow glide back in*, "filling you," *slow glide out*, "owning you." With those last words, Cade snapped his hips against his ass and filled him to the hilt.

The pleasurable sting was so intense, Daniel lost control. He threw his head back and Cade captured his cry, sliding his tongue deep inside his mouth in a claiming kiss. All he could do was breathe, and he didn't know how he was doing that.

Skin to skin, sweat to sweat, breath to breath, Cade moved over him in a hypnotizing rhythm, in and out, until Daniel gathered his wits and began to move with him, but as soon as he thought he'd regained an ounce of control, Cade twisted his hips, the new angle shuttling his cock over his prostate once more. Again. Again! He arched beneath Cade, a rush of pleasure racing through his veins, filling his cock until it throbbed back to life.

"Grab the lube," Cade instructed and pushed up to hover above him. "It's right there."

Daniel blinked away the lusty haze until he could see the lube beside them. His hand shook as he squeezed more than enough from the tube and gripped his cock, stroking himself in time with Cade's never faltering thrusts.

"Fuck yeah." Cade swore as he watched from above. "Let me know when you're almost there."

"I'm almost there," Daniel panted with a sigh.

Cade quickened his pace, the sound of his balls slapping against him growing louder and faster. The sight of Cade moving above him was surreal. His arms trembled as his muscles bunched and strained with his efforts. Sweat dripped from his hair and his chin, peppering Daniel's chest, the sensual sight shoving him straight to the edge.

"Grraaaah!" He tensed as his balls drew up tight. His hand worked faster between them, his need to come beyond any he'd ever experienced before.

"Stop," Cade ordered him, his words coming out as little more than a panted whisper.

"Fuck no!" He needed to come!

"Let go of your cock!" Cade commanded and forced Daniel's hand away from his dick.

Cade lowered himself against him, sandwiching his cock between them as he moved, sliding up and down, in and out, faster and faster. Daniel's muscles contracted to the point he thought his spine would snap as he came with a shout, his seed spilling between their stomachs.

"Fuck yes!" Cade's rhythm faltered. One last powerful snap of his hips and he stilled, his body trembling on top as his cock throbbed inside.

"So good," Cade panted, his arms giving out. He collapsed atop Daniel in a breathless heap, his face buried in the crook of Daniel's neck. "I knew you'd be the end of me," he said. "I knew it the second I saw you."

Daniel closed his eyes and wrapped his arms around him, their hearts beating together at the same rapid pace, only layers of skin and bone between them. He didn't know what to do or say. Even if he could speak, there were no words to describe what was happening to him.

He was lost.
He was Cade's.
He was fucked.

Chapter Eight

Cade paced the confines of the room, his bags already packed and waiting by the door. The ink on their new assignment still wet, his team had left an hour ago, but he'd stayed behind. As many times as he'd told himself he would, when the time came, he couldn't leave without saying goodbye.

He'd known from the start he'd have to walk away eventually, but he'd never imagined it would be this difficult, this impossible. Any distance he'd thought he'd kept between himself and Daniel was nothing more than a blatant lie he'd told himself over and over until he'd believed it to be true. He needed Daniel like he needed air to breathe, but he had no other choice. This was the life he'd chosen, and Daniel could no longer be a part of it, no matter how much he wished otherwise.

Footsteps echoed in the stairwell. He paced to the window and looked down at the street. Daniel's refurbished Jeep was parked at a crooked angle along the curb, confirming his arrival before Cade heard the knock on the door.

"Come in." He didn't turn to offer a greeting, his gaze fixed on the street below as he remembered all the great times they'd had in that Jeep—memories he'd take with him and replay every day until they faded into the background noise of life.

"Hey," Daniel said from the doorway, his questioning tone scraping along Cade's raw nerves. "What's going on?"

Resigned to their fate, Cade turned and faced him. "I'm leaving."

Daniel glanced down at the bags on the floor, his head bobbing in understanding. "Um…Okay," he said with a shaky breath, the shocked expression on his face tearing at Cade's insides. "When? I mean…soon obviously, but—"

"Now." His instincts and training told him to make a quick break, end it and walk away so they could both move on, but he couldn't. He unfolded his arms and paced over to Daniel, taking his crestfallen face between his hands. "We both knew this day would come."

Daniel swallowed as he stared back, searching for hope he wouldn't find. He jerked away from Cade's hold and took a few steps away. "Yeah, I guess we did." Daniel shoved his hands into his pockets, staring at the floor as he toed one of the warped boards with his shoe. "When will I see you again?"

Cade's chest ached as he forced himself to say the words. "You probably won't."

Daniel gave him another jerky nod. "Okay," he said with a breathy sigh. "I guess..." He turned and looked around the room as if checking for anything he might have left behind. "I guess that's goodbye then."

Cade hated himself for doing it, but he took Daniel's face into his hands again, refusing to let him go when he tried to turn away. With a desperation he'd never felt, he pressed his lips to Daniel's one last time, hoping beyond hope for one last taste.

Daniel pushed at his chest, but Cade held firm, claiming his mouth, backing him against the wall. With nowhere else to go, Daniel released a broken sigh and opened to his insistence, their tongues meeting in one last farewell kiss.

As it had been from the beginning, his need for Daniel overwhelmed his sensibility. When Daniel untucked Cade's shirt from his pants and reached for his zipper, he didn't protest or push him away. He hadn't planned to fuck him. He didn't want to drag this out, or cause more pain than he already had with a long goodbye he hadn't the time for, but he was helpless to resist. He'd give Daniel whatever he needed to dull the pain he saw in his eyes—pain he'd caused.

Daniel broke the kiss and turned him around, shoving him facedown onto the bare mattress in the middle of the floor. Not a word was spoken as he stripped Cade's pants down his hips, his hands working feverishly to unbuckle his own. With little more than spit and a condom, Daniel penetrated him, the stabbing sting in his ass obliterating the pain that had occupied his chest since the second he'd learned he was leaving. He was thankful for the distraction. He needed it. He deserved it.

There was no doubt Daniel meant to hurt him. He welcomed it. The bruises he was sure to bear from Daniel's punishing grip wouldn't last long enough to justify what he'd done. He'd known it would end this way and did nothing to stop the affection that had formed so quickly between them.

He closed his eyes and took whatever Daniel gave, the sheer force of his thrusts betraying Daniel's desperation to hold onto whatever shred of their affair he could. It was in that moment Cade wished he hadn't used a condom. He wanted to know what Daniel felt like, no barriers between them, whatever the risk.

Each powerful drive of Daniel's hips brought new pain that he bore without protest, using his memories of their time together to distract him. Another thrust. Another memory: Daniel's sarcastic laugh, his fidgety nervousness, his shrewd bright-blue eyes, the look on his face when he'd fucked him the first time—none of them erasing the memory of the hurt in his eyes when he walked in and realized their time had come to an end.

Daniel's silence vanished with his final thrust. Cade's cock was flaccid, but he relished the sound of Daniel's cry as he came inside him one final time and then collapsed against his back.

In the light of dusk, they laid together, breathless and still hurting inside, until the light faded. He'd missed his flight, but he would catch another. He owed Daniel whatever time he needed to say goodbye in whatever way he chose. If they never spoke again, it was enough.

Daniel stirred and pulled out, but when Cade tried to roll over, he pressed a hand to the middle of his back. Daniel's soft lips caressed the skin between his shoulder blades in a series of penitent kisses that trailed up his spine. Cade soaked in every one of them, committing the feel of them to memory before Daniel pressed his lips to the back of his head, lingering there as he took one last breath. "I'm sorry," Daniel whispered before he pushed himself off, the loss of contact like a final blow.

The faint sound of the door clicking closed was one Cade would remember for the rest of his life—the sound of the end of the best thing that had ever happened to him.

Chapter Nine

Present Day

Daniel stared at the third email he'd been typing to Jonah as Cade napped on the sofa. His thoughts were a jumbled mess, bouncing from Jonah to Cade to the phone call they were waiting for, when an unexpected notification popped up on his screen, the words *Hi Dad* in the subject line. He smiled as he clicked open the email.

New Message
From: Thalia G. Kendal
To: Daniel Gregory
Subject: Hi Dad

Sorry it's been a while since my last email. Thomas goaded Grant into a climbing trip to celebrate his birthday, and we've had no signal for the last two weeks. These two are going to be the death of me. I never thought I'd say this, but I'm getting too old for this stuff.

We just reached base camp and should be back in Nepal tomorrow. I'd like to come see you soon, and Thomas wants to visit his grandfather before he leaves for his next trip. It's still strange to think of you as *Gramps*, by the way. Anyway, I know calving season is a busy time, but we'd hoped to come next month. Think about it. I miss you and will call you when I have enough of a signal to make the connection. Please wish Gabby a belated happy birthday for us.

Love you,
T

Daniel laughed out loud, his heart filling with joy. His daughter was coming to see him! He resisted the urge to use her given name as he hurriedly typed out his reply. To him she would always be Natalie, his little girl he'd once thought he'd lost forever. He'd grown accustomed to calling her Thalia in the years since they'd been reunited, as she'd requested, but he would always think of her as Natalie. She was a grown woman now, married with an adopted son of her own, and he couldn't be more proud. And she was coming to Falcon Ridge! In what seemed like a never-ending storm of disappointment and anxiety, this was the best news ever.

After clicking send, he sat back in his chair, his smile uncontainable as he remembered the first time he'd laid eyes on his little girl.

Langley, Virginia – 1986

A swirl of colorful leaves danced in the wind around the front door of the coffee shop as Daniel reached for the handle. Autumn had arrived, and with it a much anticipated break in the summer heat wave that had lingered longer than usual.

Once inside, he shucked off his blazer and fell into step behind the last person in line, studying the specials as he waited. A hot cup of coffee in hand, he found a table for two near the back and grabbed the seat that offered the best view of the front door.

He'd been back stateside for six months when his ex-girlfriend, Nicky Baxter, called and asked to meet him. Talk about a blast from the past. He hadn't seen her since his last leave from Germany more than two years ago, and he certainly hadn't expected her call.

They'd first met at the video store where he'd exchanged the last copy of *Top Gun* for her phone number. She was cute, and he'd liked her a lot, until he met her so-called friends. Their short affair had ended outside the county jail, where he'd forked over what was left of his savings to bail her out after a night of partying.

He'd believed for a while he could help her, get her off the shit she was using, but when she got into his car outside the jail, and the first thing she did was hit him up for more money and a ride to her dealer's house, he was done. He'd driven her to the local hospital, checked her in, told her it was over and left her there.

When she called out of the blue a few days ago and asked him out for coffee, he'd noticed her edgy stutter was gone—the one she'd get when she was high. Maybe she'd gotten clean after all. He sipped his coffee as he waited for her to arrive. His thoughts never far from Cade, he couldn't remember if he'd ever told him about her.

After their less than dignified goodbye in Germany, three months passed before he saw Cade again. He wasn't sure at the time if it was the worst or best day of his life, but when Cade called him from Turkey and told him he was on the next flight to Frankfurt, he'd dropped everything and met him at the airport.

They spent the next eighteen hours fucking and catching up until it was time to say goodbye again, except this time with the knowledge that they'd see each other again. Cade was as incapable of staying away as he was of saying goodbye for good.

Over the next several months Daniel planned every day of his life around receiving a phone call or a letter that rarely ever came. He saw Cade twice more before he was offered an early transfer back to the States. Having no way to contact him, Daniel was hesitant to accept the transfer, but ultimately did. Cade would find him when he surfaced from his latest mission.

Six more months passed. No calls or letters. Every morning he awoke with a physical ache in his chest, knowing it was over, but unable to make himself believe it enough to move on with his life. There were times, those fleeting moments right before he woke, when he could still smell Cade's aftershave. Those days were the hardest.

The café door opened and he looked up from his cup of coffee, recognizing Nicky's ebony hair and pixie face, and a…a toddler on her hip? Once inside she paused, glancing around the room until she found him, offering him a shy wave as she made her way to their table. With every step she took, his heart rate increased, stopping altogether when she reached the table and he saw his own eyes staring back at him.

"Hi Dan."

He heard his name, but was so enthralled with the little girl in her arms he'd forgotten where he was, who he was. Nothing else existed as he reached out and ran his finger along the girl's soft little arm.

"Her name is Natalie." Nicky turned and offered her to him. Gripped with shock and so many questions he couldn't possibly comprehend them all, he reached out and took the child into his arms. When Natalie reached up and touched his face with her little hand, he was lost.

"I didn't know any other way to tell you," Nicky offered, sinking down into the chair beside them. "She looks so much like you, there was never a question, but I couldn't find you after I got out of the hospital."

No. There was no question Natalie was his. She had the same lips, the same nose, and, without a doubt, she had his crystal-blue eyes.

"Out of desperation, my attorney made some phone calls and managed to track you down."

"How old is she?" He caught the bit about her attorney, and he'd get back to that later, but right then all he could think about was the beautiful little girl in his arms. His little girl.

"She'll be three in January."

He did the math in his head in record time, not that he needed to.

"Dan, I'm in trouble."

Everything changed that day.

Nicky had been busted on a trumped up shoplifting charge and was looking at sixty days in county lock-up, but she was clean, and had been since the day she found out she was pregnant.

He fired her attorney, hired a new one who got the charges dismissed, moved her and Natalie into his apartment, filed for his release from active duty, secured a job as a U.S. Marshal and married Nicky two months later.

He didn't love her, and he'd admit his life was more complicated than he'd ever imagined it would be, but marrying her was the easiest decision he'd ever made. He still missed Cade so badly it hurt more days than not, but he wouldn't trade being a father for a million days with his former lover.

One week before they were scheduled to close on their first house, he came face to face with the ultimate test of that resolve.

He pulled into the parking spot in front of his apartment, like he did every day after picking Natalie up from the babysitters. This time, however, he found himself staring through the windshield at Cade

Candelle leaning against his front door, his ankles crossed, his hands shoved into his pockets, his crooked smile resurrecting all the feelings he'd managed to bury in the same shallow grave as his hope of ever seeing him again.

"Cowboy," Natalie said in her tiny voice from her car seat behind him, snapping him back to reality.

"Yes, the man is wearing a cowboy hat." A cowboy hat that made him look ten times sexier than he remembered. He cut the engine and got out, unstrapping Natalie from her seat and settling her in his arms before he turned and faced Cade.

"Come in," he offered instead of *hello*. It took a concerted effort not to reach out and pull Cade into his arms as he walked past him and unlocked the door.

Once inside, he settled Natalie in front of the television and flipped on her favorite cartoon before he returned to the kitchen where Cade was waiting.

"Want a drink?" he forced himself to offer. He wanted more than anything to be able to rewind the last half hour and take Natalie for the ice cream she'd asked for, instead of driving straight home. Nicky would have been home by then and would have either clued him in on their newlywed status, or at least provided a buffer.

"No thanks," Cade said, looking out of place in the small domesticated space Daniel had called home for the last year. "Why didn't you tell me you had a kid?"

"I didn't know." He didn't face Cade as he spoke, concentrating on filling his glass with ice and whatever juice was in his refrigerator.

"That…must have been quite a surprise," Cade said when he didn't offer any further explanation.

"What are you doing here, Cade?" It was a stupid question, but he couldn't ask the myriad of other ones for which he so desperately craved the answers. Why didn't you call me? Why didn't you write? Where have you been? Did you fall in love with someone else? Why can't you let me let you go? No matter what answer he gave, it wouldn't change anything. It couldn't. There was more at stake than just his heart this time.

"I know I don't deserve it, but I was hoping—"

"Hoping for what? You could come here and we'd pick up where you left me?"

"Yes," Cade said unapologetically. "I'm back in the States, now. The agency is building a new Counter Intelligence Center and I've been tapped to head up one of the divisions."

Daniel closed his eyes and tried to breathe. No matter how many times he'd told himself it was over, some small kernel of hope remained, threatening to grow into something he couldn't control if he gave it even the slightest chance. He'd given Cade that chance once, but he couldn't do it again. He needed to end this once and for all.

"I'm married." When Cade didn't respond, Daniel turned to find him staring back, studying him.

"How long do you think *that* will last?"

He'd faced a lot of different emotions over the last year. Most of them he'd managed to shove into a box so far back in the closet he could almost forget they existed, but the anger that boiled up inside him was insurmountable. How dare he come back after all this time and expect him to leave everything: his wife, his life, his *daughter*!

"This is over," Daniel said with as much restraint as he could manage. He marched to the door and opened it, daring Cade to challenge him.

Cade stood rooted in place long enough to make him wonder if he would argue, but eventually capitulated with a nod. He stopped in the doorway and looked up at him with the same green eyes that ghosted in and out of his dreams almost every night. "I came to see you in Germany, right after you left."

Daniel swallowed against the knot in his throat. Regret gripped his chest so tight it threatened to suffocate him. Cade hadn't left him. If he'd stayed in Germany… If he hadn't come home, he wouldn't have Natalie. A piece of him died in that moment, knowing what he could have had, and that he wouldn't change his decision even if he could. Despite his anger, he needed Cade to know he hadn't left him.

"I waited over a year for you," was all he could manage before his voice cracked.

"I understand." Cade leaned in and placed a gentle kiss to his lips. He tensed at the unexpected contact, every fiber of his being fighting like hell not to kiss him back, not to pull him back inside and fall apart in his arms, not to beg him to stay. Out of all their goodbyes, this was the hardest.

Cade broke away and placed a finger over his trembling lips. "Do what you need to do. I'll be waiting for you."

Weeks went by before he felt like he could breathe again. The months passed in a blur. He and Nicky slipped into a comfortable routine, but things had changed. He'd changed. Depression was a constant battle. He loved Natalie with all his heart and tried to make that enough, and most days it was.

Nicky sensed the loss acutely. They fought over every little thing, sometimes just for the sake of fighting, and he couldn't bring himself to tell her why. He worked longer hours, taking cases that kept him away from home when he could, putting more of a strain on his relationships with both his wife and daughter.

The strain proved too much for Nicky. On his way home one night he received a call from the hospital. The babysitter had found her passed out on their bed, unresponsive from the drugs she'd taken. Drugs she'd been taking for months.

Looking back, he should have seen the signs. She'd lost weight, started drinking again. At first only at social gatherings, but he'd noticed the empty bottles in the trash at home in recent weeks. The edginess in her tone was back, but he'd written it off as stress. She'd missed picking Natalie up from school three times in the last two weeks. *God, had she been high when she did pick her up?*

Nicky's relapse was a wake-up call. They couldn't go on as they had been. He either needed to be in his marriage or out of it, and every time he looked into Natalie's eyes he knew the answer.

Nicky checked herself into rehab again. Things were tough for a while, but he'd made her a promise he intended to keep, and it was time he got his head out of his ass and started being the husband and father his family needed.

By Christmas later that same year, Nicky was a full-fledged addict again, and in the worst shape he'd ever seen her. When she refused to go back to rehab, he hid the keys to her car, took away her access to their bank account, and began taking Natalie to school, having the babysitter pick her up in the afternoons and stay until he got home from work. He hadn't worked an out-of-state case in months and his performance began to suffer from his lack of commitment.

He was their only source of income, and couldn't afford to lose his job. The additional babysitting fees alone were as much as their mortgage. As hard as he tried, he could feel it all slipping away again. The constant ups and downs were taking their toll and he didn't know how much longer he could keep it together.

When he got another call, this time from a local police detective he worked with, informing him that Nicky had been picked up in an undercover sting on a local dealer, while Natalie was in the car, he had to draw a line beyond hiding the keys.

The fight they'd had when his wife came home was one for the record books, but ended the instant he promised to leave and take Natalie with him. He hated using threats, especially using their daughter against her. She was Natalie's mother, but he would fight to the death to keep her safe if Nicky didn't get, and stay, clean.

The next few months were the hardest. Nicky came home from rehab, clean and sober, but the new medication they prescribed made her more of a zombie than a mom or wife. He tried to reconnect with her on some elemental level, but she couldn't find herself through the haze of the medications, much less find him.

He came home from work one day to find the house torn apart. Furniture was tipped over, dishes broken and scattered. Their clothes littered the floor from the kitchen to the bathroom. He drew his sidearm and picked his way through the mess until he got to the kitchen phone, dialing nine-one-one, thinking someone had broken in and trashed the place.

"Nicky!" He called through the house, but heard nothing. When he reached the end of the hall, he pushed his daughter's door open with his toe, his gun drawn. He peered inside to find Natalie sitting on her bed, huddled in the corner by the wall.

"Nattie, honey?" He rushed over and pulled her into his arms. "Are you okay?"

"Mommy's mad," she said in a whisper.

"It's okay, sweetheart." The air rushed from his lungs in relief as he re-holstered his gun. He cradled her to his chest and wiped away the tracks of dried tears from her chubby cheeks.

"Where's mommy?" he asked in the calmest voice he could manage. Natalie pointed to their room across the hall. He sucked in a deep calming breath and set her back on the bed, reaching over to retrieve her favorite doll from the pillow. "Stay here and talk to Molly for a minute. Find out if she wants ice cream or cookies after dinner, and I'll be right back, okay? Can you do that for daddy?"

Natalie gave him a silent nod.

"Good girl." He kissed her forehead before he left the room, closing the door behind him.

Once in the hallway, he heard Nicky's faint whimper coming from their room. He followed the sound until he found his wife sitting on the closet floor, weeping,

"Nicky? What's wrong?" His heart stopped when she looked up at him. Her hair was a tangled mess. Black mascara ran down both her cheeks with the tracks of her tears. Her pupils were blown and her whole body shook as she fought the waning effects of her last hit.

"You never loved me," she said and stared down at the piece of paper in her hand. "Not like this."

He froze when he saw the box he'd hidden Cade's letters in, lying open in her lap.

He thought to deny it, but couldn't make himself tell her another lie.

"All this time I knew something wasn't right. I thought it was me."

"Nicky, no." He knelt on the floor in front of her and tried to pull her into his arms, but she pushed him away.

"You lied to me!"

"I didn't lie, Nik. I just…couldn't tell you about that part of my life. I've never told anyone." *Jesus!* He'd never expected to have this conversation with her, and to do it with her in this condition...

Nicky shook her head and sucked in a steadying breath, her hands trembling as she wiped away her tears. "You've been seeing him, haven't you?"

"No," he vehemently denied the accusation. "I've never cheated on you. I swear it. Not with him or anyone else."

She was quiet for so long, fear settled like a hot rock in the pit of his stomach. What was she thinking? If she left him he'd have no choice but to fight her for custody of Natalie. *Oh God, Natalie.* He couldn't imagine what this could do to her. As fucked up as Nicky was, she was still her mom and Natalie needed her.

"Nicky, we need to get you to the hospital. We'll talk about it when you're sober."

"No!" Nicky tossed the letters aside and pushed up from the floor, stumbling into what was left of their hanging clothes. "I'm leaving," she said with a whimper, shoving him away when he tried to help her.

"You can't leave like this, Nik! You're high. We need to talk."

"I can't!" she screamed from the hallway moments before the front door slammed behind her.

Nicky never came back. After three days with no phone call or messages, he called the police and filed a missing person's report. She surfaced a few weeks later at the county hospital with an overdose and checked herself back into rehab when she was released. A few months later, he was served with divorce papers and an order to appear for a custody hearing, at which Nicky didn't bother to show. After several delays and countless more hearings, their divorce was granted and he was awarded full custody of Natalie.

He'd tried to locate Nicky, but she'd dropped off the map, until she called him early one morning a year later from the Alabama State Pen, asking for money to hire another lawyer. This time she was arrested on possession with intent to sell, and there was nothing he could do to help. Natalie was twelve by the time she was released. He never heard from Nicky again.

In a way he was grateful. He'd built a good life for Natalie and he didn't want it poisoned with Nicky's addiction. There was a part of him, however, that would always blame himself for Nicky's relapse. Cade had been right. If he'd loved her the way he should have, if he'd been the husband she'd needed, she might have found the strength to be the mother Natalie deserved.

It was that same guilt that kept him from accepting Cade's invitation to join him in Montana after his divorce. Ever the spook, Cade had kept tabs on him throughout the years. They talked on the phone sometimes, mostly on holidays and a handful of unexpected occasions.

He both loved and hated those calls. Hearing Cade's voice was like a balm to his weary soul, but each time they talked, he had to fight that much harder not to lose what was left of his heart.

Cade never stopped asking, though. Daniel continually refused, citing every excuse in the book: his job, Natalie's school, not wanting to uproot her life and take her away from her friends. In truth he couldn't stomach the idea of explaining Cade to Natalie. He couldn't be *that* person in his daughter's eyes, couldn't face that side of himself and the loss of control Cade represented. He'd managed to find a happy medium, a life he could be proud of, even if he was only superficially content in the world he'd built for his daughter.

When Natalie was abducted three years later, his comfortable world completely collapsed.

D.L. Roan

Chapter Ten

Burning alive in the deepest pit of hell. That's the only way Daniel could describe the hours following Natalie's abduction. When she drove to school that morning, her first solo trip with her new driver's license, he could never have imagined it would be the last time he saw her.

"I've already called all of her friends!" he shouted at the officers in his living room, resisting the overwhelming urge to punch them both. They weren't listening! "She wouldn't do this! Not today. She knew how nervous I was about her driving herself to school. And if you suggest one more time that she ran away, I'll shove that pen you're pretending to write everything down with up your ass!"

"Calm down, Daniel," his boss said. "We have our entire team out looking for her."

Daniel shoved his boss's hand off his shoulder with a curse and paced to the front window, hoping to see the flash of her headlights as she pulled into the driveway. The longer he stood there, the more he knew something was wrong. *Where is she?*

Minute by minute, her ten o'clock curfew came and went. Midnight loomed and he paced the confines of the living room. "I can't stay here," he said and marched to the front door, ripping his coat from the coatrack and shoving his arms into the sleeves. "I need to be out there looking for her."

His boss's cellphone rang. Daniel's grip tightened around the front door handle as he listened to him talk, waiting on the edge for any scrap of information.

"I see," his boss said, holding up a finger for Daniel to wait. "Thank you. I'll let him know." Daniel was numb by the time his boss hung up the phone and shoved it back into his pocket with a disappointed sigh. "Nicky's in California. She doesn't have her."

The doorknob twisted beneath his grip and Daniel opened the door. "Mr. Gregory." One of the local deputies stood on the other side, his eyes betraying his efforts to temper the news he'd come to share. "We found her car." Daniel knew by the way he spoke that she wasn't in it. His insides began to shake as the deputy continued. "It was pushed into the woods up by the water tower. It looks like she had a flat tire on the way home from school. Her purse and phone were found inside, but there's no sign of her."

He'd never felt more helpless, though it was far more than just a feeling. Not knowing where she was, or what happened to her, pushed him to the brink of madness and then shoved him right over into a never-ending abyss.

Every day after that was spent in a cloud of numbness and despair, wandering through the responsibilities of his job as he mapped out another area of the city to search. The nights were a daunting mix of driving the streets looking for her, and battling back nightmares of every possible horror she could be enduring. When he slept.

He landed in the hospital a month later, exhausted, dehydrated, thirty pounds lighter from consuming nothing but coffee and antacids every day. Something had to change, so he took leave from his job and devoted every moment of his time to finding her.

A break in the case came three months after she disappeared.

"Do you recognize any of the girls in these photographs?"

Daniel stood in the hallway outside the detective's office as the young girl inside looked over an array of pictures of missing girls, one of them Natalie's. The girl had been abducted a month before Natalie and managed to escape her captors, blowing the lid off a local sex trafficking ring. Torn between hope and despair, he strained to hear her voice as she spoke. If they got a positive ID, they'd have an official direction to look, but the idea of his little girl being abducted by sex traffickers was a fresh new kind of hell.

"This one," she said. Daniel's heart seized. "She was there."

"Are you sure?" the detective asked.

"Yes," the girl insisted. "I remember her blue eyes." The pressure inside Daniel's head swelled, the ringing in his ears drowning out every other sound as he tried and failed to hold himself together. "She fought them at first," he heard her say, "but they drugged her and took her away."

"Where did they take her?" the detective asked.

"I don't know!" The girl began to cry and her parents ended the meeting, ushering her out of the office.

Daniel stood paralyzed in the hallway and watched them walk away, taking the remains of his hope with them.

A few hours later he stared at the half-empty fifth of whisky in his hand. He couldn't feel the neck of the glass bottle clenched in his fist, but the ache in his chest was still as acute as it had been when he started drinking, so he tipped it back and guzzled another long swig. When he lowered the bottle, the room began to spin, but when he closed his eyes, all he could see were the sick images of what those monsters were doing to Natalie.

"How could you let this happen?" he shouted into the darkness of his daughter's bedroom. He'd never gone to church or read the Bible, but he'd always believed there was something more, bigger than the world could explain, protecting and watching over them. How could God do this to her?

When no answers came, he rolled from her bed and stumbled over to the dresser, the whisky bottle falling from his hand as he reached out and picked up the blue ribbon hanging from her MVP trophy. He caressed the satin with his thumb as he remembered the day her volleyball team had won the regional championships.

She'd been the star of the game, scoring more points and blocks than he could count. The match was tied and he could still feel the excitement in the air as he watched her approach the net. Her teammate gave her the perfect assist and Natalie jumped into the air, delivering an indefensible spike to the ball, scoring the winning match point.

Daniel jumped to his feet in triumph, shouting with the other fans as Natalie celebrated the win with her teammates. She caught his eye and gave him a wave before she ran over and jumped into his arms. He hugged her tight and spun her around, laughing with pride and joy as they celebrated her win. All too soon she let him go, and he looked down to see her smile fade away, her eyes widening in fear.

"Nattie, what's wrong?" He reached out to pull her back to him, but she stumbled backwards, a stranger's hands grabbing her from behind and pulling her into a sea of people.

"Natalie!" He pushed through the crowd, but couldn't reach her.

"Daddy!" She clawed at the hands that held her, but couldn't get free. "Daddy, help me!"

The sound of Natalie's scream snapped him from his memory. He stared through his tears at the ribbon in his hand, his gaze wandering to the whisky bottle on the floor, a puddle of amber liquid staining the carpet beside it.

"I can't do this."

He shoved the ribbon into his pocket and picked up the bottle. The hallway tilted and swayed as he walked to his bedroom and retrieved his pistol from the nightstand. The bathroom light glared like a hazy beacon in the distance, illuminating his steps as he traversed his way across the room. The whisky bottle clanged against the bathtub as he climbed inside, shattering into a dozen jagged pieces and spilling the remaining contents onto his lap and down the drain.

"Shit." He stared at what remained of the bottle in his hand before he tossed it over the edge of the tub. None of it mattered anyway. In a few minutes it would all be over.

Broken glass crunched beneath his palm as he settled himself against the back wall of the tub, intent on saving the coroner's office the trouble of picking his brains up off the floor.

When he raised the gun to his mouth, he saw the cut on his hand. A thick crimson trail ran down the inside of his arm to his elbow, drops of blood splashing onto the white porcelain tub beneath him.

Any pain he might have felt from the cut was eclipsed by the gaping hole in his chest. He'd once thought himself strong enough to handle whatever life threw at him, but not this. This kind of pain was unbearable.

He opened his mouth and shoved the barrel between his teeth, his breath rushing in and out as he stared down at the trigger. He could do this. One twitch of his finger and the pain would end.

He closed his eyes and slid his thumb to the trigger.
Daddy!

Natalie's scream echoed against the tile behind him and he jerked the gun from his mouth. When he opened his eyes, all he saw was himself, sitting in a pile of broken glass and blood.

"Fuck!" He slammed his head against the wall behind him and raised the gun to his mouth again.

Daddy, help me!

"Shut up!" he screamed at his daughter's ghost. He raised the gun again, his hand shaking so violently the barrel of the gun clinked against his teeth. His stomach lurched and he squeezed his eyes shut, his chest heaving in and out with his final breaths. Adrenaline pumped through his veins, providing the first blessed hint of the numbness he sought, but he couldn't do it. No matter how hard he tried, he couldn't pull the trigger. He couldn't leave her to those bastards. He couldn't bear the thought of what might be happening to her, but he couldn't help her if he was dead.

His sobs stole his resolve. He let the gun fall from his grasp, over the edge of the bathtub, before he curled into a ball among the broken glass, and wept until he passed out.

Sunrise came, its bright rays piercing his drunken haze. His head pounded as he forced himself up and out of the bathtub, stumbling into the kitchen to clean and bandage the cut on his hand.

Once the blood flow stopped, he pulled his cellphone from his pocket to see if he'd missed any calls, something he did on autopilot what seemed like every ten minutes, hoping to see Natalie's name on the caller ID. It was a stupid habit, because if she did call, it wouldn't be from a number his phone would recognize, but he hoped anyway. It was all he had left.

He didn't know if it was a result of his snooping, a sixth sense he possessed, or some twisted kin to fate, but Cade's name appeared on the missed call log. His fingers pressed the callback button before he'd even processed the urge to hear his voice.

"Are you okay?"

"No," Daniel said, his voice scratchy and hoarse. "I...I can't..." His legs gave out and he slid down the wall beside the overflowing trashcan onto the tile floor, a fresh flow of tears stinging his eyes. "If I'd come to Montana when you asked me to, she would still be..." he sobbed into the phone, unable to finish.

"You don't know that," Cade insisted. "Don't you dare go borrowing trouble, Daniel. This is not your fault."

"It *is* my fault! Goddammit!" He punched the trash can beside him, sending it and all its rancid contents skittering across the kitchen floor. The action did little to relieve his grief and more tears flowed unchecked from his bloodshot eyes.

"I'll be on the next flight out of Billings."

"No!" Daniel nearly puked at the thought. He might puke anyway, if the room didn't stop spinning.

"Dammit! Let me help you!" Cade's voice roared in his ear.

"I said no." Daniel scrubbed his forearm over his eyes and cleared his throat, determined not to crumble. "I can't...I can't see you. Not right now." If he had to deal with Cade on top of everything else, he would break. Saying goodbye to him again would kill him, and there was no way he was going to leave Virginia now. If Natalie somehow survived, or escaped and came home, he needed to be there for her. "Please don't."

Cade's silence spoke volumes, but he lacked the emotional bandwidth to address it. He struggled his way through the details of what they'd found. If Cade wanted to help, he could find someone competent to assist him in looking for Natalie.

"I'll make some calls," Cade promised. "But if you need me, I'm always here. Do you understand?"

Daniel nodded silently. That was half his problem. Whether he was there or not, Cade was *always there.*

"Daniel! Promise me you won't do something stupid."

"Yes, okay. I won't."

"I'll call you back."

The line went dead. He stared at the phone in his hand until the dial tone turned into a loud, irritating buzz, snapping him from his dead-headed daze. He plugged the phone into the charger, took a shower, put on a fresh change of clothes, and went back to searching for Natalie. He knew it was pointless. The probability she was even still in the States, and not some third-world country on the other side of the world, was miniscule—if not hopeless—but searching was the only thing he had left.

Through his contacts at work, and help from Cade, he was introduced to a former victim's advocate who worked for the International Crime Investigation division of the FBI in St. Louis, Missouri.

Rebecca Danes was a young agent looking for her break-out case, and he liked her on the spot. She was hungry, passionate about her job. He believed her when she said she'd find his daughter. As Rebecca dug into Natalie's case and began looking for her, Daniel went to work finding the bastards who took her.

Having exhausted his leave, he returned to work. While slogging through his official cases, he waged an all-out war on every underground crime organization that even smelled like it dabbled in human trafficking. He'd come up with a handful of leads, but nothing stuck until the Feds busted a street thug working for a slime lord named Hector Morganti.

Morganti was known as an enforcer for the drug cartels, but their snitch suggested it was a cover for the fortune he raked in smuggling kids into an underground sex trafficking ring.

After a year-long investigation, Daniel was more certain than ever that Morganti was responsible for Natalie's abduction. He'd even heard rumors about a ledger he kept of all the victims he trafficked and to whom—the sick bastard. If it existed, Daniel needed to get his hands on that ledger. He would hunt down and kill every single monster who ever laid a hand on his daughter.

The Feds worked the case until they uncovered a trafficking network that spanned the globe, bigger than any of them ever imagined, with Hector Morganti at its helm in the States. But their case against him was weak, until they hit a break and cut a deal with Morganti's daughter.

Gabriella Morganti was a young, innocent-as-they-come heiress to one of the biggest crime syndicates on the east coast. She was clueless about her father's crimes, but held enough pieces to the puzzle: Morganti's whereabouts on certain dates, people he trusted, connecting the dots the Feds couldn't, to put her father away for life, and Daniel planned on using that information to find Morganti's ledger.

After Morganti's arrest, Gabriella was placed under federal protection. As they waited for her father's trial to begin, Daniel forced himself onto her protection detail, intending to get as close to her as he could. He didn't like using her, but he needed every ounce of information he could gather if he had any chance of finding Natalie.

One of the first things he learned was Gabby's visceral fear of a man named Lucien Moretti, her father's second in command. A Brooklyn reject, Lucien had come to work for Gabby's father when she was but a girl. Her youth had been an attractive quality to Lucien. He'd fixated on her and was determined to have her, one way or another. Gabby's father had picked up on Lucien's obsession and used it to his advantage, holding her far enough out of Lucien's reach to control him.

Unbeknownst to Gabby, her father had struck a deal with Lucien— a deal that would see Gabby handed over to him on her twenty-first birthday, without question or concern for her wellbeing, in exchange for Lucien's unconditional loyalty. That deal had been Morganti's undoing.

When the day came to cash in on the bargain her father had struck, Gabby was called to his study where Lucien waited. With a twisted grin on his lips, Lucien had demanded she strip off her clothes, then tried to rip them from her body when she refused. She'd screamed in horror, pleading with her father for help, but he'd only stood there, watching as Lucien tried to force himself upon her.

Gabby's only brother had heard her cries for help and rushed into their father's study. Her memories of what happened after Lucien was pulled from atop her were vague at best. She'd tried to stop Lucien from hurting her brother, but in the chaos of flying fists, was shoved to the floor and hit her head on the corner of her father's desk. When she came to, her brother was lying dead in a pool of his own blood, and the room was full of crooked cops.

When Lucien tried to tear her away from her brother's body, she'd screamed and kicked, fighting with all she had until her father finally intervened. Unaware of the Fed's investigation, Morganti gave her a choice: go with Lucien peacefully, or he'd have her arrested for her brother's murder. Gabby had chosen jail, and then turned state's evidence when the Feds offered her a deal.

Unfortunately for their case, Lucien had kept himself as clean as a whistle during his time with Morganti. The bastard was untouchable in the indictment, but he had the one thing Daniel needed to find Natalie. Morganti's ledger of victims and clients was never found, and Daniel had no doubt it was in Lucien's possession. If Daniel was going to find Natalie, and the bastards who bought her, Lucien and that ledger would be his best hope. He needed Gabby to get his hands on both.

Trading Gabby for that ledger hadn't been a part Daniel's original plan, but as the months passed, and not one shred of evidence was produced in Morganti's trial to lead him to Natalie, the temptation became more than a passing thought. During that time, however, Gabby became less like a potential source to get to Lucien, and more like a daughter to him. Every day he awoke and began a fresh battle with his conscience. If he handed her over to that monster, killing her would be the least of the atrocities Lucien would inflict on her. If he didn't, he may never find his daughter or the bastards who'd hurt her.

But Gabby was innocent. She was good and kind and having her in his life had given him back some of the humanity he'd lost when Natalie was taken from him. He was no longer dead inside and he had Gabby to thank for that.

"Drink your tea," he urged her as he sat on the edge of her bed. She'd had trouble sleeping since her father's trial began and he'd made a habit of steeping a cup of chamomile tea every night before she went to bed.

"When will this be over?" she asked with a tired sigh. "It's been a year."

"I don't know." He motioned for her to take a sip. "The wheels of justice are slow, but they're still turning." He glanced around the room, taking in the various pictures hanging on the walls. "At least this place has style." They were lucky to have working plumbing in some of the safe houses they'd stayed in.

Gabby swallowed another sip and nodded. "Thank you," she said and took his hand. "I don't know what I would do if you weren't here with me."

Daniel gave her hand a squeeze. "No need to thank me."

"I'm just sorry I couldn't help you more with Lucien," she said cupping her hands around the warmth of teacup.

The trial took three long years to conclude. His relationship with Gabby progressed beyond his ability to reason away his thoughts of giving her to Lucien. He couldn't betray the memory of his daughter, and he'd be doing just that if he allowed his grief and need for revenge to destroy Gabby, too.

When Morganti's life sentence was imposed, the danger to Gabby's life didn't end. Lucien still wanted her and Daniel knew he wouldn't give up until he found her. Her agreement with the Feds included a new identity and a fresh start, but when they pulled her protection detail after the trial ended, Daniel couldn't abandon her. He retired from the U.S. Marshals and made the most difficult phone call of his life.

"I need your help," he said when Cade answered. They hadn't spoken since the trial began. Cade had every right to hang up on him, and Daniel half expected him to, but he didn't.

"Do we need a secure line?" was Cade's only response. "If it's illegal, I'd recommend it."

"Yeah, something like that," Daniel said with a nervous laugh. Cade may have left The Agency, but The Agency had never left him.

"I'll call you back." Cade hung up before Daniel could give him another number. A few seconds later, the burner cellphone in his back pocket rang.

"I don't even want to know how you did that," Daniel said when he answered it.

"You're right. You don't." Cade's sharp tone allowed no room for questions. "What's up?"

"I need a place to hide Gabriella Morganti. The feds gave her new credentials, but Lucien Moretti is still searching for her. I have a plan, but I need someone I can trust to help me execute it."

Cade didn't answer immediately, a reaction he'd come to expect. "*Do* you trust me?" he finally asked, the tone in his voice asking more than the words themselves.

Daniel sucked in a long breath and released it with a resigned sigh. "I've never *not* trusted you," he said as he paced the confines of their hotel room on the outskirts of Pittsburgh. "It was me I didn't trust. Never you."

"What do you need?" Cade asked after another long pause.

Daniel sank down on the edge of the bed, the knot in the pit of his stomach relaxing as he revealed his plan. "I want to lure Lucien into a trap, but I have to know, without a doubt, Gabby will be safe. She can't know anything about this or it will never work. She's a nervous wreck already and, if she suspects anything, she'll blow the last chance I've got to catch Lucien."

"You want me to keep an eye on her?" Cade asked. "You know I can do that best if you bring her here, right? We'll have the home field advantage."

Daniel closed his eyes and imagined what it would be like to see Cade again. Did he still have that crooked smile that made the rest of the world disappear?

He was eager for a break from the harsh reality of his life—a reality filled with evil and grief and regret. He needed to feel wanted and alive, in a way only Cade could make him feel. His goal was to protect Gabby, but he needed Cade in ways that surpassed every other human need, and he'd finally reached a point in his life where he was no longer afraid to admit it.

"I miss you." The words were like water to a starving plant, dulling the ache in his chest. "I don't know what else to say or do, but I know this is the right thing, for me and for Gabby."

He didn't know if the sigh Cade released was one of relief or disbelief, but when he said he'd do whatever he could to help, it gave Daniel more hope than he'd had in a decade. "We'll figure it out when you get here, okay?"

"Yeah, okay," he choked out. "Thank you."

"Do you have someone on the inside working with you?" Cade asked, moving their conversation from the awkward end of the spectrum to the business part of his plan.

"Um, yeah, I do." He peeled the curtain back to look for his friend. Not seeing any signs of a new vehicle in the parking lot, he let the curtain fall back over the window. He paced to the other end of the room as he debated what to tell Cade, deciding full disclosure was his best option. "He'll be going by the name of Grant Kendal when he meets with you."

Cade half chuckled-half snorted. "One of those, huh? You like the secret spy types, I see."

"Oh, no! It's not like that!" Daniel rushed to reassure him. *Dammit!* How had he screwed this up already? "He's a former colleague from work. I trained him—I mean—I helped, but there's nothing personal. And then The Agency picked him up. I don't know what he does now, but we didn't—we never—"

"I was pulling your chain." Cade snickered. "You never could take a joke."

Daniel cursed as he gulped for air like a dying guppy, his heartbeat racing. "Fuck you."

"I've missed you, too," Cade said with a laugh.

The easy tone in his voice took Daniel back to the time when they first met—getting high on the rooftop of his shitty apartment building, laughing and fucking and sleeping in each other's arms until the sun came up the next morning, and he'd get up and rush through his day so they could do it all over again. He'd thought that feeling was gone, but with four little words, it all came back and he remembered why it had been so easy to fall in love with Cade.

"I'll call you back when I have all the details worked out on this end," Daniel said and hung up the phone. The sooner he could put his plan into motion, the sooner he would see Cade, and *hot-damn* it couldn't be soon enough.

Chapter Eleven

"It's time."

Daniel paused in front of the mirror, one hand holding his razor against his cheek, the other clutching the phone in a death grip as he waited for Cade to say more. So far everything had gone according to plan. Cade had secured Gabby a job as a substitute teacher in the small town where he lived in Montana, and Daniel had sent her on her way.

He'd second-guessed not telling her about their plan a thousand times, but caution had eventually won the battle against his guilt. He let her go with the belief that she was finally on her own. It was best she think it was over, and go about starting her new life as if it were.

As innocent as Gabby was, she was incapable of subterfuge, and if she knew about their plan to lure Lucien to Montana, using her as bait, she'd fall apart the second Lucien's thugs arrived to verify her identity; she'd blow the whole op. Hell, he'd been a walking wreck himself since the moment she'd left their roadside motel room in Pittsburgh, where he'd stayed behind to wait for word from Cade.

The second Cade confirmed that Gabby's location had been successfully leaked to Lucien, Daniel'd caught the first flight to Billings and checked into a small Bed and Breakfast in the town just south of where Cade lived, where he'd been waiting for Cade to confirm that Lucien was on his way.

"Is he there?" Daniel asked in the wake of Cade's silence.

"One of his aliases popped up on a flight to Billings. He'll be here the day after tomorrow. I don't know how long it will take him to locate her, but we shouldn't take any chances."

"I'll be there in an hour," he said as he wiped the stray traces of shaving cream from his face. "I'll tell Grant to meet us at your place so we can go over the plan."

"Grant is a piece of work by the way," Cade said with a chuckle. "That part of the plan worked seamlessly. He's pulled the wool over my nephews' eyes with his 'handyman' act."

"Is Gabby staying there, too?" At the mention of Cade's nephews, he began to second guess their plan. In the short time Gabby had been in Grassland, Cade's nephews, Grey, Matt, and Mason had begun dating her. All *three* of them. He didn't know how to feel about the idea of three men and a single woman in a relationship together. How serious could it be?

"Yes," Cade answered, "and she doesn't suspect a thing as far as I can tell. You were right about her. She's as skittish as a newborn colt. My nephews have taken her in, but they got a little suspicious when I started asking questions about her, so I've kept my distance."

"Is she going to be okay?" Daniel asked. "I mean, I don't want to see her get hurt. Three brothers after the same woman...I can't see that working out too well in the end."

"Don't worry," Cade insisted. "If there's one thing I've learned from watching her, she knows how to take care of herself," he argued. "You taught her well. Besides, you know my sister is married to three brothers, and has been for more than two decades. They've managed to make it work."

"Yeah, but—"

"Reserve judgment until you get here and meet them," Cade insisted. "You might be surprised. And we have bigger fish to fry right now," he reminded Daniel. "Stay focused on the plan, Boss."

Daniel nodded, grinning at the familiar cocky tone in Cade's voice. "You're right. I just..." He looked at his watch, his stomach growling from the late morning hour with no sustenance. "I'll be there soon."

"Daniel?" Cade said as he was about to hang up.

"Yeah."

"I can't wait to see you again."

And just like that, anticipation stirred back to life in his gut. He hadn't seen Cade since his unexpected visit to his apartment in Virginia more than a decade ago and he was beyond nervous.

He released a sigh and glanced up at himself in the mirror one last time. He was still trim and fit for a man closing in on middle-aged. *Mostly.*

"Me too," he said and closed his phone. He leaned closer to the mirror and ran his hand over his greying flattop, checking to make sure he hadn't missed a spot shaving. "Me too," he said again with more hope than conviction, before he turned out the light and made quick work of packing his things.

By the time he pulled into the long, gravel driveway at the address Cade had given him, he was a nervous wreck and second guessing everything. What if Cade was only interested in another fling? What if he'd already found someone else but hadn't told him? What if they'd missed something and Lucien managed to get his hands on Gabby? What if-what if-what if!

His hands trembled as he parked in front of the old country house and cut the engine. Instead of getting out, he sat in the car, struggling to breathe. This was it. There was no turning back. In a few seconds he would see Cade again and, no matter what happened between them, he needed to hold himself together for Gabby's sake.

The front door opened. The shadow beneath the wide porch roof concealed Cade's figure, revealing him inch by inch from his boots up as he walked to the edge of the porch, until he appeared at the top of the steps, illuminated by the midafternoon sun.

Daniel's lips parted on a hopeless sigh, the air in his lungs rushing out with a whoosh. Cade looked the same as he remembered: lean and narrow-hipped, tan-skinned, thick sandy-colored hair—much shorter than it used to be—flapping in the breeze against his forehead. He walked with the same carefree, confident gait as he ambled down the steps, making Daniel want things he hadn't dared allow himself to want for so long.

As Cade reached the bottom of the steps, Daniel unfastened his seatbelt and stepped out onto the driveway, hiding his trembling hands by shoving the keys deep into his pockets. Standing beside the car, he held his breath, not knowing what to say or do, unable to look away from Cade's unreadable expression. He never could read the man. He guessed that would never change.

With only a few steps between them, he noticed the collage of changes he hadn't been able to see from a distance. Fine lines gathered at the corners of Cade's eyes and lips. Strands of silver in his hair—barely noticeable—glistened in the afternoon sun. Cade had a few years on him, and now that he could see them, those years looked damn good.

Unexpected guilt rose inside at the time they'd lost—time he'd wasted pushing Cade away. His chest burned with the need for oxygen as Cade stopped in front of him. His heart pounded against his ribs, echoing in his eardrums. Sweat stung his skin and dampened his shirt as another wave of nervous anxiety bubbled to the surface. He died a hundred deaths as he waited for the man to speak. Do something. Anything.

Cade reached out, took Daniel's face between his hands and kissed him. In the blink of an eye, all of his concerns vanished. The feel of Cade's gripping touch, his lips, the silky slide of his tongue alongside his own, his familiar taste, the sound of the gravel shifting beneath their boots as they struggled to stand beneath the crushing weight of so many days gone by, all blended together into a euphoric high like none he'd ever felt before.

All of the denial and grief, pain and guilt, love and longing he'd battled back year after year, burst from somewhere deep inside with such force he didn't think about who may be watching, or what anyone else thought. He wrapped his arms around Cade and hugged him with an ardent grip, kissing him back with a passion that threatened to overrun all of his senses at once.

Cade pressed himself deeper into the embrace, crushing him against the car, chasing—claiming more than ever before. Daniel gave him everything he demanded. Visceral and raw, their kiss melted away the years between them and all that was left was what truly mattered. He belonged to Cade, and Cade hadn't given up on him.

Sweaty and breathless, the intensity of their reunion simmered to a slow boil. Cade melted against him. He loosened his grip, but couldn't force himself to let go.

He roamed his hands over Cade's body, reacquainting himself with the feel and taste of the man he loved. Every touch was a test of reality, to make sure he wasn't dreaming. He caressed Cade's chest, his back, down over his ass, pulling him closer until he felt Cade's hard cock against his own. When Cade groaned against his lips, he smiled. He couldn't help it. The feeling of happiness was so foreign it tickled his insides. This was real.

"Like I said," Cade chuckled, pressing his hard cock against Daniel's, "I've missed you, too."

He sounded drunk, his words slow and lazy. Daniel felt drunk as he pressed his forehead to Cade's and tried to string together a coherent reply. He couldn't. All he could do was breathe, and smile, and soak in the feel of Cade in his arms.

Cade cupped his hands around Daniel's face and commanded his gaze. To his relief, he looked down to see him smiling, too.

"We have a lot of time to make up for."

Daniel nodded, feeling a stab of guilt, but Cade caught it and his grip tightened. "Don't," he insisted, his smile fading as his eyes narrowed. "I didn't mean it like that. You're here. That's all that matters."

He swallowed, surrendering his guilt to the feel of Cade's lips moving against his in kiss after exploring kiss, until they were both breathless once again and he allowed Cade to pull away.

"We need to talk before Grant arrives," Cade reminded him, reaching down to take his hand.

"Yeah. Shit." Cade had kissed him so senseless, he'd forgotten the other reason he was there—the most important reason. "Grant said he needed to finish up a job for your nephews and he'd be over around four." He checked his watch, wondering how much making up they could do in an hour.

"Let's get your things and go inside. I have something I'd like to show you."

Cade's mischievous wink as he grabbed the bag from the back seat set Daniel's bones on fire, just as it always had. Cade took his hand again and led him up the front steps. He stared at the white-washed threshold. The second they stepped through that door, it was unlikely they'd do much talking, and there were a few things he needed to say.

"Wait." He tugged Cade to a stop.

The sound of gunfire echoed in the distance. Cade spun around and peered at the line of trees running along the valley behind his house. Several more shots rang out.

"Fuck! Something's going on at the ranch!" Cade rushed into the house and Daniel followed.

"It can't be Lucien. He's not due in for two more days."

"I don't know what's going on, but that's not buckshot." Cade opened a closet near the front door and retrieved a rifle. "Stay here and let me check it out."

"The hell I will! Gabby's there!"

"She can't know you're here," Cade reminded him. "If she sees you, she'll know we're up to something. She doesn't know me, but being related to the men she's dating is an easier explanation than why you're here. It could be anything. Poachers, maybe. We have to stick to the plan until we know for sure. Grab a beer from the fridge and take a load off. I'll be right back."

Cade gave him no time to argue, leaving him standing in the doorway as he hopped into his pick-up and took off down the driveway, leaving nothing but a trail of dust in his wake.

Daniel pulled his phone from his pocket and dialed Grant's number. The call rang until it rolled over to voicemail and he dialed it again. He tried it three more times with the same result.

"Dammit!"

Daniel slammed the front door and found his way to the kitchen, opened the refrigerator and stared sightlessly inside without a clue of what he was doing, or what he was supposed to do next. The contents of the refrigerator came into focus and he slammed the door. Eating or drinking was out of the question.

He paced to the window and looked outside, taking a calming breath. Cade was right. He was in Montana. People owned guns, and there were a lot of reasons they would use them. Feeling the weight of his own sidearm on his hip added to his calm and he relaxed a fraction, taking in the feel of Cade's home.

He wandered from room to room, looking but rarely touching. The pictures of his family, the antique furniture, the warm and inviting sunshine filling the living room, were all at odds with the memories of the ramshackle hotel room he'd associated with Cade throughout the years. This was his home. This was where his heart lived. This was where Daniel wanted to be, too, more than anything.

He reached out and plucked a photograph from a line of many others sitting on the mantel above the fireplace. In it, a young version of Cade stood beside a younger woman, three other men gathered around her on the other side. He assumed the woman was his sister,

Hazel, and her three husbands. His smile faded as he thought of Gabby and Cade's three nephews. Could she be happy in such a relationship? He wasn't one to judge if it's what she truly wanted, but he couldn't help but want to protect her.

A picture at the end of the row caught his eye. He reached out and took it from the mantel, his fingers playing over the glass-covered image. It was Gabby, laughing with two little boys—toe-headed twins with bright green eyes and dirt-smudged faces, their hair and shorts soaking wet from swimming in the creek behind them. Cade had told him about his nephews' first wife dying in childbirth, leaving his nephews to raise the boys—Connor and Carson he believed their names were—on their own. His chest ached with the happiness the picture conveyed. *Cade must have taken it while he was watching over her*, he thought as he studied Gabby's face. He hadn't seen her smile like that even once in the years he'd known her.

The loud ring of Cade's home phone echoed through the quiet house. He fumbled the pictures in his hands, catching one against his chest and the other inches from the floor. He laid the pictures on the coffee table and followed the sound into the kitchen. While he debated answering the call, the ringing stopped, eliminating the decision to invade Cade's privacy and possibly reveal his presence. Not a smart move.

"I need to get a grip, for God's sake." He jerked open the refrigerator and snagged a beer, twisted the cap off and took several long gulps. The cold brew was tart and invigorating. He carried the bottle into the hallway and stared up at the top of the steps, wondering if Cade's bedroom was upstairs or down. Hopefully, everything was fine and he'd find out soon enough, but he didn't feel comfortable snooping.

The sun was setting by the time he heard the sound of gravel crunching beneath tires. He abandoned the three empty bottles on the coffee table and rushed to the front door, peering out the small window in the top to verify it was Cade, and that he was alone, before he opened the door. Cade's expression was as unreadable as ever, but the purposeful way he walked across the driveway and up the stairs left no doubt something was wrong.

"What happened?"

Cade shook his head. "Let's talk inside."

"What the hell happened?" Daniel insisted, jerking him to a stop. "Is Gabby okay?"

Cade took a deep breath, unable to meet his gaze. "Gabby's been shot, but it wasn't Lucien."

Chapter Twelve

Present Day

"What are you thinking about?" Cade asked, laughing when Daniel jerked in his chair and threw his hand over his heart. "Sorry, I didn't mean to startle you."

"The hell you didn't," Daniel choked out. "You love doing that shit."

"You're going to drive yourself mad sitting here waiting on the doctor to call," Cade said, leaning against the doorframe. "I told you not to worry."

"I wasn't." Daniel glanced at his laptop. "I was thinking about the day Gabby was shot."

Cade's smile faded. "That's not much better." With whatever news was headed their way, the last thing Daniel needed was to be thinking about *that* day.

Unbeknownst to Cade, or anyone else for that matter, the principle of the school where Gabby taught when she first came to Grassland had been off his rocker. Propelled by some form of religious insanity and prejudice against his family's polyandry, he'd convinced himself that little Connor and Carson were some sort of demon spawns and had tried to kill them, shooting Gabby instead when she attempted to save them. Decades later, Cade was still confounded at how a lunatic like that could have gotten a job running a private school.

"That day wasn't all bad, though," Daniel argued, reminding him of their reunion. He propped his head on his fist and winked lazily. "And everything turned out okay in the end."

In the end. Cade wondered if they weren't already near the end, and the clock was ticking, but Daniel didn't know about his suspicions. His stomach soured and lurched at the thought of telling him. He couldn't. Not yet. He gave Daniel a practiced wink instead. "I'm going to run over to Con and Car's place for a bit."

"Oh, okay. I'll go with you," Daniel offered, closing his laptop.

"No you won't. It's your night to cook," Cade insisted, pulling the truck keys from his pocket. He needed time to gather his courage, and he hoped beyond hope Connor and Carson's wife, Breezy, would be able to help him. "I'll be back in a few, and I'll expect to smell your legendary spaghetti sauce from the road when I get here."

"It's Gabby's recipe, not mine," Daniel argued, his brows knitting together as he tried to figure out what Cade was up to. Daniel had learned to read him over the years, but there were still times he could sneak under his radar if he tried hard enough.

"And that reminds me," Daniel continued. "Natalie emailed me. She and Thomas are coming for a visit next month."

"Good." He was going to need his daughter and grandson more than ever soon. "That's great." Cade leaned down and gave his lover a kiss. "I'll be right back."

"Let me know if the doctor calls!" Daniel shouted as Cade grabbed his coat and made his way to the door.

"Spaghetti!" Cade yelled back before the door closed behind him.

He glanced up at the grey sky, the cold air biting through his thin coat. *Perfect weather for shitty news.*

By the time he reached the other side of Falcon Ridge, his dark mood had deepened. The quick nap he'd taken hadn't helped. Each day proved longer and more draining than the previous. The pain had been manageable for the last few weeks, but he'd crossed some invisible threshold and he felt like his body was giving out.

He slowed his truck to a stop on the side of the long driveway a few hundred yards from his grandnephews' house. Overlooking Falcon Ridge, he sat and stared out the windshield at all his family had built. Acres upon acres of beauty, even in the midst of the winter freeze. He'd spent his youth running in those fields, fishing in the creek, climbing the rocky faces of the surrounding mountains.

Falcon Ridge had always held a magic he could never fully explain. Even now, he could still feel that magic coursing through his veins, but it was leaving him. His body was failing him, he was sure, forcing him to leave Daniel.

"Dammit all to hell!"

He wasn't supposed to be the first one to go. Yeah, he was older, and he couldn't fathom losing Daniel first, but he didn't want Daniel to feel the pain of loss again. Fate had already dealt him enough grief for one lifetime.

When Gabby was shot by that lunatic, he'd thought Daniel would come unglued. For three days he watched as his friend and one-time lover climbed the walls, waiting for news of her recovery. Not being able to see her tore him apart, but with Lucien on the prowl in Grassland, they couldn't take the chance.

Cade and Grant took turns standing watch for Lucien outside the hospital as the rest of his family came and went. As Gabby's condition improved, he could no longer ignore his sister's persistent questions about Grant and their odd behavior in the time of crisis. They needed to tell his family the truth about Gabby and her past, and why she was in so much danger. He'd wished it could have been under different circumstances, but it was time they meet Daniel, and understand why they'd brought Gabby to Falcon Ridge in the first place. With Lucien so close, he needed them all as far away from the hospital as possible.

He'd called a meeting with his sister, Hazel, and her three husbands, introduced Daniel and explained Grant's role in their plan. He'd never told his family about Daniel, but Hazel had known, from the time he'd come back home to Falcon Ridge, that he'd been waiting for someone. She'd taken one look at Daniel and understood everything.

Her husbands and his nephews, on the other hand, had not. They'd been spitting mad when they learned Cade and Daniel had brought that kind of danger into their lives.

Cooler heads prevailed, however, and Daniel told them his story; how he'd met Gabby, who her father was, why Lucien wanted her. He'd been visibly shaken as he described the day his daughter had been abducted and the ledger he needed to find her. Daniel sacrificed a lot for Cade that day, dredging up memories that cut deeper than even he'd imagined. Cade had stood in awe of him, understanding for the first time the suffering he'd endured through the years he'd searched for Natalie.

Daniel's story proved too much for Hazel to bear, and she collapsed with chest pains. Their mad dash back to the hospital seemed like a nightmare, but the second they arrived, Daniel's cellphone rang and bad turned to worse. When he spoke Gabby's name into the phone, Cade looked up to see one of Lucien's men standing guard near the front lobby.

"Stay here, Grey." Grant shouldered Cade's nephew back as one of the elevator doors opened and they stepped inside. "Stay with your family and tend to your mother."

"Like hell!" Grey pushed his way back through the closing door. "What the *hell* is going on?"

Cade pushed his way inside the elevator before the doors closed. "I spot two at the main entry and one near the stairs."

"Two what?" Grey asked.

Cade reached out and clasped his nephew's arm. He understood Grey's concern for Gabby, but he didn't have time to explain what was happening. Nor did he want to lose another family member today. God, he prayed Hazel would be okay.

"Lucien is here," he whispered to Grey.

Daniel continued to speak calming words through his phone to Gabby as Grant turned his attention to the phone in his hands. "Keep her talking, Daniel. We've got a tracking app on her phone. We'll find her."

Cade closed his eyes and prayed the application code his friend had given him worked. It was a new technology, not even on the market yet, and the tests he'd run before installing it had produced less than stellar results.

"Where are you?" Daniel asked Gabby as Grant pushed the button for the third floor. "She's in an office," he said. "She doesn't know where."

"She's on three," Grant barked as he palmed his phone and drew his .45 from his shoulder holster. "You take the right," he told Cade as the elevator slowed. "Daniel and I'll take the left wing and we'll meet at the other end of the floor. Check every room and keep your back to the wall. Lucien won't be alone."

It was difficult for Cade to leave Daniel's side, but he knew he was capable of taking care of himself, and he'd grown to trust Grant.

Cade shuffled down the hall. As he checked each room, he shooed away the nurses and doctors, ordering them to leave the building. When he turned the corner, the sound of a woman's scream echoed around him, followed by an eruption of gunfire.

Adrenaline pumped through his veins as he sprinted into the fray, parting the sea of fleeing hospital staff and patients, tripping over discarded clipboards and an overturned gurney. He stopped at the corridor, his gun drawn, but before he could check to make sure the connecting hallway was clear, his nephew ran past him towards Gabby, who was lying on the floor a few dozen feet away.

"Grey, no!" His warning was too late. Another shot was fired, striking Grey in the leg as he bounded past him.

"See to Gabby!" Daniel rounded the corner after Grant, both hot on Lucien's heels before they all disappeared behind the stairwell door.

Nurses and doctors rushed to Grey's aide. Confident in his care, Cade did as Daniel asked. He knelt in front of Gabby, taking her trembling hands into his own, wincing at the blood seeping from the bandages on her shoulder. He didn't know if the blood was from her first wound, or if she'd been shot again. "Help!" he cried out to the group of doctors working on Grey. "Over here!"

"Grey?" Gabby's brows pinched together as she studied him with a frantic gaze, her eyes glassy and bloodshot. "Who are you?" she slapped at his hands, pushing him away. "Grey!"

"Sit tight, Gabriella," he said as he checked for any signs she'd been hurt again. "As soon as Daniel gives me the okay, I'll get you back to your room and get you some help."

"You know Daniel? M…Marshal Gregory?"

"My name is Cade and yes, Daniel is my friend."

"Uncle Cade! Is she hurt?" Grey shouted from the end of the hall. He turned to see the nurses cutting away Grey's jeans and shirt before they loaded him onto a gurney.

"Grey!" Gabby tore herself from Cade's grip and bolted to her feet. Her legs crumbled beneath her and she fell to her knees. "Grey! You're hurt!" She scrambled across the floor toward him. "Oh God! Grey. I'm sorry! I'm so sorry! I never meant for this to happen!"

Cade held Gabby, sobbing in his arms, as they wheeled Grey away to see to his wound. Judging by the amount of blood on the floor, the bullet had hit an artery. He prayed a silent prayer that Grey would be okay. His family would never forgive him if he wasn't.

Several nurses appeared at his side and he handed Gabby over to them, standing watch as they helped her to an empty room and checked her over. Relief poured through his veins when they found no new injuries except for a few torn stitches and some bruises. With the help of the sedative they'd given her, she was sleeping peacefully when Daniel found her room thirty minutes later, his face ashen with shock and exhaustion.

"Did you get him?" He crossed the room and took Daniel by the shoulders, checking him over for any injuries.

"Lucien's dead," he said with little emotion, shouldering past him to Gabby's bedside.

"She's fine," Cade assured him. "She tore open her stitches and got a little banged up in the scuffle, but she's okay."

Daniel stood with his back to him, staring at Gabby's sleeping form.

Cade reached out to lay his hand on his back, but the tension rising in the air between them gave him pause. Daniel was about to break. Though Gabby would be okay, if Lucien was dead it meant he would never find Hector Morganti's ledger. He may never find Natalie without it.

For the first time in Cade's life he didn't know what to do or say. He didn't have a quick-witted joke to offer, or a soothing string of words at the ready to distract him. If he said or did the wrong thing, he could lose him, and this time it might be forever.

"Mr. Gregory? Cade?"

He turned to see the Sherriff at the door, two of his deputies at his side. "We need the both of you to come down to the station to speak with our detectives."

"Can't this wait?" he argued.

"I've got a hospital full of bullet holes and a dead man in the stairwell, Cade. I need some damn answers before the Feds start crawling up our asses."

"It's fine," Daniel said, his tone flat and lifeless. "Let's go."

Hours, hell maybe even a whole day passed before the Sherriff let them go. Streaks of red and gold cut across the summer sky, the day fading into dusk as they crawled into his truck and pulled onto Main Street.

"Hazel called while I was in the bathroom washing up," he said, unsure if Daniel would even hear him. Though he'd given direct answers to the detectives, he hadn't spoken a word to Cade since they'd left the hospital. "Grey's going to be okay, and Gabby is still sleeping. Do you want me to take you back to the hospital?"

Daniel shook his head, but didn't offer an alternative, staring out the window in continued silence.

Daniel was still in a daze when they reached Cade's house, his eyelids heavy with exhaustion and what Cade guessed was shock. When Daniel didn't make any attempt to get out, Cade cut the engine and stepped out of the truck. He walked over to Daniel's door and opened it, taking his hand and guiding him through the motions until he was standing on his own two feet. Like a lost puppy, he followed in Cade's wake as he climbed up the front steps, opened the door and led him to the second floor bathroom.

Cade flipped on the hot water in the shower, letting it fill the room with steam as he undressed Daniel and then himself. They hadn't kissed or even touched since the day Gabby was shot. Their reunion had ended as quickly as it had begun. Cade didn't know if what he was doing now was right or wrong—if it crossed some line between loving him and taking advantage. All he knew was that Daniel was hurting. He'd never stopped hurting.

Cade had been godsmacked the day he'd visited Daniel in Virginia and learned of the new life he'd begun. He'd also seen the toll his abandonment had taken on Daniel. He'd been on assignment, but that was no excuse. There were opportunities to write or call. Plenty of them. He simply chose not to. He'd thought, at the time, letting Daniel go was the best thing for them both. He should have known he'd never be able to erase him from the pages of his heart's story. Their story.

Seeing him again, kissing him, holding him, deepened Cade's resolve to see their reunion through to the end. If their story ended today, he'd know he'd done everything he could to give Daniel the love he deserved.

At Cade's urging, Daniel stepped over the threshold into the steaming spray. Cade followed, closing the shower door behind them. He picked up a bar of soap and worked up a thick lather between his palms before he reached out and laid his hands on Daniel's broad back.

With languid, loving strokes, he caressed the spot between his shoulder blades, placing a kiss on his heated skin before moving to a new, untouched place on Daniel's body: one shoulder, then the next, his thick chest, his left flank, and then his right. He loved and kissed him until Daniel began to tremble beneath his touch.

Daniel braced himself against the shower wall, his head hanging between his outstretched arms as the water poured over his back. A single mournful sob broke free, then another, each shaking him to the core.

Cade draped himself over his lover, wrapping himself around him, holding him together as best he could as Daniel cried. "Let it out," he coaxed as he kissed his back, his neck, any and every place he could reach.

"I'll never find her." Daniel's grief-stricken cry echoed off the tile walls.

"It's okay," Cade repeated between kisses, his lips trembling as he spoke. He didn't know if the words were true, but for as long as he lived he'd do his damnedest to make them so. "You'll be okay."

Daniel's knees buckled and they crumpled to the shower floor together. Cade gathered him in his arms and held him as the hot water rained down around them, drowning their tears as Daniel mourned the loss of his daughter, and his last thread of hope of ever finding her.

The next morning Cade woke with the sunrise, as was his custom, but something was different. He opened his eyes and the memories flooded in like a summer storm.

Daniel had cried in the shower until he'd made himself sick. Cade had stayed by his side until there were no tears left to cry, and then dried them both off and took Daniel to his bed. They'd both drifted off to sleep some hours later, Daniel's body tucked seamlessly against his own—right where he belonged.

He turned and looked at Daniel lying next to him. His eyes were closed, his lips parted in slumber. Had it all been a dream? He reached out and caressed his cheek, releasing a quiet breath of relief when he felt the stubble against his fingertips.

As he remembered what it felt like to kiss him there, Daniel's eyelids fluttered open. His ice-blue gaze met Cade's, and his heart stuttered.

"Good morning," Cade said, unable to contain his grin despite his worry. The night had been long and full of grief. "How are you feeling?"

Daniel blinked and rolled to his back, scrubbing his hands over his face with a growl. "Like shit," he said, staring up at the ceiling.

Cade remained silent, allowing him time to gather his thoughts. For the first time since they'd met, he couldn't read the man. With everything that had happened with Gabby and Lucien, everything personal between them had been put on hold. They hadn't discussed their relationship, their past, their future, none of it. Saying goodbye to Daniel again would rip his heart out, but he couldn't let him see that. The man had enough to sort out. As much as he wanted to take him into his arms and make love to him, he had to give him time.

"I'll find a way to survive," Daniel continued. "I always do. I'm just sorry you had to see that last night."

Cade pressed his fingers to Daniel's lips. "Don't be sorry," he whispered. "Say anything else you want, but don't be sorry."

Daniel reached up and cupped Cade's cheek, his lips turning up into a lazy morning smile. "Thank you," Daniel said, his voice a raspy rumble that raked along Cade's spine, straight to the morning hard-on he was trying desperately to ignore. "Thank you for helping me save Gabby, but most of all, for never giving up on me."

Cade couldn't resist. He rolled atop Daniel and kissed him, hard and long. Daniel's familiar scent filled his nostrils as Cade breathed him in, pressing their bodies together beneath the sheet. "I'll never give up on you," he said as he kissed along his jaw, relishing the feel of his stubble against his lips.

"Promise?"

The question in Daniel's voice made him pause. He drew back and looked down, finally able to read the look in his eyes. Hope was not lost. Neither were they.

"Never."

He kissed and nipped along the strong tendons in Daniel's neck, over his collarbone, his thick chest muscles before he took one flat nipple between his teeth and flicked it with his tongue. Daniel arched beneath him, his next breath hissing between his teeth. He watched him through his lashes as he moved to the other one, biting a little harder this time.

"Ahhh!"

Cade grinned and licked away the biting pain. "I remember how much you love that."

Daniel's response was another groan as Cade dipped lower and took his cock to the back of his throat. Cade closed his eyes and savored the firm, silky feel of his lover, the salty taste of his pre-cum tempting him to draw out more. Memories that had kept his hope alive blended with the reality of having Daniel in his bed again, making him dizzy. The years without his touch made him drunk with lust, the combination sending his body into a rioting frenzy of need.

The sounds of Daniel's pleasure, the sight of the tendons in his neck straining tighter with every torturous flick of his tongue or flip of his wrist, added to his high, pushing him closer and closer to the edge.

Determined to be inside Daniel when he came, Cade doubled his grip and hollowed his cheeks, sucking him deep one last time before he pulled back, tonguing the rim of his head the way he knew would pull Daniel right to the precipice, teetering, swaying, fighting not to come because it felt so damn good he didn't want it to end.

"Fuck!" Daniel's hips left the bed as he came, his fists gnarled in the sheets, every muscle in his body taut and quivering with his release.

Cade swallowed every drop, savoring his lover's taste as he watched Daniel come apart beneath him. He couldn't wait another second.

"Turn over," he ordered as he reached for the tube of lubricant he kept on the bedside table, eying the condoms, but deciding to leave them where they lay.

Daniel turned over onto his stomach and Cade parted his legs, revealing his dark puckered hole. He gripped his ass cheek and ran his thumb along the rim, debating whether or not to kiss him there before he fucked him. Daniel loved a good rimming, but his pleading moan told Cade it would have to wait.

He squeezed out a generous amount of lube and worked it inside Daniel's ass with his left hand as he lubed up his cock with his right, the tandem rhythms making his heart beat faster with anticipation, his hips flex with shameless need.

"Now," Daniel demanded and pressed back against Cade's hand. "I don't want to wait another second."

He didn't need another second. Cade gripped his hips and pressed the tip of his cock against Daniel. "I'm not wearing a condom."

If he said no, he'd use one, but he wanted more than anything to feel him, all of him, with no barriers between them, latex or otherwise.

Daniel's answer was a cry of blissful agony as he pushed up on his arms and impaled himself on Cade's cock. Buried inside his lover's hot ass, Cade cried out as they both collapsed back to the mattress.

"Damn," he panted into the crook of Daniel's neck. He'd never fucked anyone, man or woman, without a condom. "Feels so good." His words came out as a broken slur when Daniel clenched around him. Being inside him, the heat, the tight grip on his cock, the skin-to-skin feel of his lover beneath him—it all swirled around inside him, driving him to move.

Daniel released a low, hummed groan with each slow stroke, his arms extended out in front of him, his hands fisted in the tangle of sheets and pillows as he reached for something to brace against. Cade stretched out above him and gripped his forearms, locking him beneath him. Buried to the hilt, he pumped inside him, determined to feel every inch of his body before they were done.

The muted sound of his pelvis slapping against Daniel's ass echoed in the small room, each thrust followed by a restrained grunt from them both. As Daniel opened up to him, he relaxed his grip, slid his hands down Daniel's arms and threaded their fingers together, kissing his shoulder, his cheek, the side of his neck, tonguing the shell of his ear as he made love to the man who'd held his heart and soul for damn near twenty years.

He didn't know if this would be the last time, or the first of many more. All that mattered was that Daniel was there now, beneath him, loving him, accepting his body into his own with abandon and trust he'd long since mourned and never thought he would feel again.

As the grip on his control waivered, he pushed harder and Daniel's groans grew louder. Pressing his forehead against the mattress, his grip crushing Cade's fingers with each inward stroke, Daniel finally let go.

"Uhhgh-uhhgh-uhhgh!"

The sounds that ripped from Daniel's throat fed Cade's desires, fueling his need to a fevered pitch. Daniel threw his head back, shouting a string of unintelligible curses, and Cade took advantage, nipping the outer shell of his ear as he drove his cock deep inside him, riding him with abandon.

The release of a lifetime ripped through Cade's body with visceral speed. He came with a shout, sinking his teeth into Daniel's shoulder as wave after wave of pure bliss rolled through him. Emptying himself inside his lover felt so good it hurt. Years had passed with only dreams of making love to him again. Those dreams never stood a chance against the real deal.

Breathless and sated, he kissed Daniel's shoulder, soothing the bite mark he'd left behind, and slowly pulled out, collapsing onto the mattress beside him. The light from the sun blazed through the window now, illuminating the sheen of sweat coating their naked bodies. The day looked brighter than any he'd known before. He didn't know if it was because Daniel was lying beside him, or because he'd just made love to him, but one thing was certain. He didn't want to see another sunrise without him.

Chapter Thirteen

"They seem to love her," Daniel said of Cade's nephews, three weeks of nights later as they lay on a pile of blanket-covered hay in the bed of his pick-up truck, staring up at the sea of stars. "And Gabby loves them. I can't deny that."

Cade brought their laced fingers to his lips and kissed the back of Daniel's hand. He'd never given much thought to romantic gestures like holding hands, or romantic evenings beneath the stars, but Daniel made him want those things. The man still had his quirks about public displays of affection. Neither of them were the out-and-proud type, but he'd found himself incapable of not touching him when they were alone.

"I've never seen them like this with anyone since their wife died," he said, wrangling his thoughts back to the subject at hand before he embarrassed himself.

Gabby made a full recovery, and Cade's nephews were going to propose to her soon, carrying on the family's polyandrous traditions it looked like. They hadn't said as much, but he knew his nephews. They were up to something big, and he couldn't be happier for them. "I didn't think they would ever find another woman to love—not together, the way they do."

"Your sister and her husbands do seem happy," Daniel mused. "I guess a relationship like that could work with the right people."

Cade turned onto his side and propped up on his elbow to look down at Daniel. "Can we make us work?"

The question had burned in his gut for weeks. Gabby was staying, but Daniel had made no such declaration. Sweat broke out on the back of his neck when Daniel didn't answer. He'd done his penance for walking away from them in the beginning. Waiting for Daniel to come back to him was the hardest thing he'd ever done. Now that

Daniel was there, knowing what life was like without him, he couldn't go back.

"Will you stay? With me?"

Daniel looked up at him, his expression indifferent. Cade's heart plummeted from the stars and landed somewhere in the vicinity of his stomach, the sudden crash inducing the urge to vomit. Then he saw it: the first crack in Daniel's lips as they turned up into a devious grin.

"I thought you'd never ask."

He sucked in a breath when he caught Daniel's wink, pushing himself up onto his ass. "You were fucking with me?"

Daniel laughed out loud, the sound sending Cade's heart soaring back into the clouds.

"You were fucking with me." Cade couldn't decide if he wanted to punch him or kiss him.

"I get so little opportunity for payback," Daniel said with a laugh, raising his hands in defense as Cade tackled him.

Daniel let him win. Cade pinned his forearms beside his head and hovered above him, staring down into eyes that had seen so much pain, but held nothing but happiness in that moment.

"Fuck you," he said in a whisper, memorizing Daniel's smile.

"Fuck me," Daniel whispered back, his words an invitation Cade would print and frame if he could.

The next eighteen months were the best of Cade's life. Daniel moved in for good. They slept in the same bed, woke up every morning and shared coffee, made breakfast together, worked on the ranch when his nephews needed their help, and fucked every chance they got. When they weren't fucking, they were living life like there was no tomorrow.

Grey's brother, Mason, even taught Daniel how to ride. Cade had never laughed so much or so hard in his life than the day he came back from a headcount trip with his nephew, Matt, and saw Daniel bouncing around on the back of ole' Biscuit like a rag doll in a clothes dryer. Mason didn't give up, though. He turned Cade's yankee lover into a skilled rider before the next calving season.

Gabby and his nephews got married, and soon after announced they were expecting twins. Daniel had more or less adopted his nephews' sons from their previous marriage, Connor and Carson, taking the six-year-olds fishing every chance the weather allowed. And he was over the moon about being a grandfather again.

Cade didn't remember ever being so happy. Their life was by no means a Norman Rockwell vision of the typical American family. It was so much more, so much fuller than he'd dared to dream possible, until their phone rang in the middle of the night, ripping Daniel from his arms, threatening to erase it all.

Natalie was alive.

Daniel hung up the phone and marched straight into their closet, ripping random handfuls of clothes from their hangers and stuffing them into a duffle bag.

"What happened?" Cade asked, bolting from the bed and rushing to his lover's side.

"Grant found Natalie. I have to go."

Cade wiped the sleep from his eyes and grabbed a suitcase from the top shelf. "I'll go with you."

"No!" Daniel rushed from the closet and marched to their dresser, pulling out drawer after drawer. "She's in trouble. I have to help her."

"Daniel, stop." Cade took him by the shoulders and forced him to meet his eyes. Daniel's panic was tangible, seeping from his pores and spiraling around them like a toxic fog. "Breathe," Cade said, giving his shoulders a shake. Daniel released a shuddering breath, his arms falling helplessly to his sides. "Tell me what happened."

"I-I-I don't know," he insisted. "Grant only said he'd found her, and she's in trouble." He tried to turn back to the dresser but Cade refused to let him go.

"What else?" he demanded.

"H-he's sending an email with the flight info. I have to get to Billings."

"Where are you flying to? Where is she?"

Daniel broke free from his hold and shoved a handful of socks and underwear into his bag. "Somewhere in Africa. I'll let you know when I get there."

Cade released him, tamping down the hurt that bloomed in his chest over Daniel's unwillingness to let him help. He pulled on his jeans and a worn shirt, went downstairs and cursed their broken coffee maker, grabbing two bottles of water from the fridge instead and meeting him at the front door. "I'll drive you."

Daniel didn't argue and two hours later Cade said goodbye, watching him sprint up the steps and disappear into the bowels of an unmarked jet.

Over the next week, he poured himself into whatever menial tasks his nephews gave him. Exhausted and broken, he stumbled into bed each night and woke before dawn to do it all over again. He couldn't ignore the feeling that he'd just lost everything, but if he worked hard enough he wouldn't have the energy to fuel it into more than a burning ember in his gut.

Daniel loved him, of that he was sure, but would it be enough? Cade had learned long ago that nothing could ever compete with Daniel's love for Natalie. He understood it, admired him for it even, but would there be room for them both this time?

The phone call he received a week after Daniel left offered no answers, but when Grant told him Daniel had been shot and was undergoing emergency surgery in India, Cade dropped everything and caught the first available flight out of Billings. Fresh off the ranch, he didn't shower, didn't change clothes, he didn't even pack a bag. He grabbed his passport, phone and truck keys and twenty eight hours later he was sitting in a rickshaw, his head pounding from lack of food and sleep and the fucking blaring car horns, trying to get a cellphone signal to call Grant.

"Yeah." The sound of Grant's voice on the line startled him. The phone hadn't even rung.

"Grant! It's Cade!" he shouted over the static. "I touched down an hour ago and I'm on my way to the hospital. Is he alive?"

"He's out of surgery. I think he'll be okay."

"You think? What did the doctors say?"

"I don't know. I left before I saw them."

"You left? Where are you?" After a long pause, he pulled the phone from his ear and checked the signal. "Grant?"

"Yeah, I'm…I don't know where I'm going, but I couldn't stay there. Listen, Cade…"

"I'm here," he said when Grant didn't continue.

"Daniel's daughter, Thalia, she's there. She's...uh...she's okay but she's in shock."

"Thalia? You mean Natalie?"

"Shit, sorry. Yeah. Thalia is what she goes by now. It's the name...never mind. Just...take care of her for me, okay?"

Grant's tone was somber, resolved, telling him there was more to the story, but Natalie was important to Daniel, so she was important to him.

"Of course," he said and the line went dead. Whether Grant hung up, or the call was dropped he would never know.

The rickshaw stopped in front of the hospital. He threw a wad of cash at the runner and sprinted through the front doors. After a long argument with an army of staff, where his rusty Hindi came in handy, he was permitted up to what he guessed was their equivalent of an intensive care waiting room.

"Mr. Candelle!"

He turned at the sound of his name to see a familiar face. "Rebecca?"

The redhead he'd Skyped with a dozen times over the last decade, getting updates on Natalie's case—and details about Daniel when he could—rushed over to him and wrapped her arms around him. "I'm so glad you're here."

"What are you doing here?"

"Daniel picked me up in D.C. on his way."

A sharp arrow of disappointment, tipped with a little jealousy, pricked his heart, but he ignored the pain. He understood why Daniel had asked her to come along, and he was glad she had. "How's Daniel? Is he okay?"

Rebecca nodded and ushered him out into the hall, glancing back at the dark-haired woman huddled in the corner. "The bullet missed his spine, but there's some nerve damage. We won't know how bad it is until the swelling goes down."

"Have you seen him? Can I see him?"

"No, I haven't." She glanced back at the woman in the waiting room. "I know you want to see him as soon as possible, but can I ask you to let Natalie go ahead of you? She's practically catatonic with grief and shock, and I think seeing him will help her cope with everything else that's happened."

"Is that her?" He studied the woman huddled in the chair, her long black hair hanging like a curtain, hiding her face. He couldn't fathom what she must have gone through over the years, what she must still be facing. "What the hell *did* happen?"

He sipped a cup of vending machine coffee as Rebecca filled him in. While she laid out the details of one of the most influential U.S. Senator's role in the international human trafficking organization they'd busted, and saving Natalie from him, Cade's thoughts were dominated by one key piece of her story.

Natalie had no memory of Daniel.

Even as Rebecca spoke, he stood and wandered into the waiting room, taking a seat beside Natalie.

"Hi," he said in a gentle tone, careful not to startle her. "My name is Cade." He held out his hand, but she didn't offer to take it, or even bother to look at him. He lowered his hand and picked his way through the most one-sided conversation he'd ever had.

"I know you don't know me," he said, unsure of where to start. "I won't try to guess what kind of hell you're going through, but I want to tell you some things about your father."

He rambled on for what seemed like hours about how he and Daniel met, and the first time he saw her, when she was but a toddler. He told her how proud Daniel was of her and how much he loved her. He told her about the endless hours, months, years her father had spent looking for her and exacting vengeance on the bastards who took her. He told her about the ranch and their life in Montana—every detail he could think of, even how Daniel drank his coffee. In the hours they waited to see him, he told her everything he knew and loved about Daniel.

She didn't respond or ask any questions. He wasn't even sure she'd heard a damn thing he'd said. Silence filled the small hotbox of a waiting room when he finally stopped speaking. He blew out a frustrated breath and moved to stand, his legs numb from sitting so long, when she reached out and placed her hand atop his. He paused and glanced down at her, but she didn't look up, her gaze still hidden behind her long curtain of tangled hair. She threaded her fingers with his and gave his hand a reassuring squeeze.

"Family for Daniel Gregory?" a feminine voice called out in a thick accent from the end of the hall.

His gut tightened. Natalie released his hand. "You can go," she said, her first words to him since he'd arrived.

Every cell in his body wanted to take her up on her offer, but he knew Daniel. "No," he insisted. "He won't rest until he sees you."

Natalie didn't move at first, but eventually unfolded her long legs and pushed from her seat. Her first steps were hobbled, and he noticed the bandages on her thigh and ankles. He watched as she limped away, but before she reached the doorway, she turned to face him.

"Thank you," she said. Cade's lungs ceased to work, the similarities so surreal it stole his breath. She looked like a supermodel version of Daniel, but her eyes were what reached out and grabbed his heart. She had Daniel's eyes, so ice-blue they shimmered.

Daniel looked exhausted by the time Cade saw him an hour later; the longest hour of his life.

"I'm sorry I didn't call y—"

Cade bent down and pressed his lips to Daniel's, unable to contain his need to touch and claim him, but scared if he touched anything else he might break him. A sigh rushed from his lungs the second their lips met, his relief so acute his body trembled with it. "I told you before," he whispered between kisses, his voice trembling as he spoke, "don't say you're sorry."

Several weeks later he, Daniel and Natalie—or Thalia, as she requested they call her—returned to the ranch, but life was nothing like it had been before they left, and none of it was easy.

Daniel required several more surgeries and months of physical therapy before he would walk again. Natalie shut down completely. Even with the help of an army of psychologists, she struggled to adjust to the new life they tried to provide for her.

When they woke one morning to find her room empty, a letter on her pillow the only sign she'd been there, Cade wasn't sure how Daniel would react. He didn't know what to say to take away the emptiness in his eyes as he took the letter into his office and closed the door.

They'd overcome so much, but there was a small place inside Cade's heart that still harbored a fear of losing Daniel—losing them. There was a time, in the arrogance of his youth, he'd thought himself unbreakable. Age and the trials of life had cured him of that naivety. No man was unbreakable, least of all him.

He didn't know what the letter read, or what Daniel was doing with it. All he could do was wait, and hope, and pray. He busied himself around the house until there was nothing left to do, then sat vigil outside the closed door until the sun set and Daniel emerged.

"She needs to find herself," he said with quiet resolve. "I found my way back to you, and she'll find her way back to me when she's ready."

Cade bolted to his feet and wrapped himself around Daniel. "She will," he promised, holding his lover as tight as he could, desperate to give him the strength he needed to believe his own words. "She will."

Natalie had been damaged in some fundamental way, but she was tough. She came from good stock. He believed, he prayed, she would emerge even stronger from whatever hell she was going through. And he'd been right.

Natalie wrote many letters to her father over the next months, some of which were nothing more than post cards from various places around the world. But each one changed Daniel, some giving him strength, others nurturing his hope of her return.

When Natalie called Cade and asked for his help to get her back into the States undetected to visit Daniel, he had to make it happen. As a result of what happened in India, she and Grant lived their lives with targets on their backs, on the run from international thugs and governments alike. He'd worked with Grant for months to cut through miles of red tape and keep her visit a secret. He was determined to do this for Daniel, and what better moment to reunite them than Christmas morning.

Chapter Fourteen

Sitting beside Daniel in his nephews' living room, surrounded by the tempting aroma of Christmas dinner cooking in the kitchen, Cade watched his audacious family swim in a sea of presents.

Gabby reached toward the back of the slowly dwindling pile of unopened gifts and retrieved a small, neatly wrapped box, handing it to him. "That one's for Daniel."

"Careful, Daniel," his nephew, Grey, warned. "You might want to check the name tag on that," he said, giving Gabby a salacious wink.

Cade rolled his eyes and handed the gift to Daniel. He'd grown accustomed to his nephews' overt flirting with their new wife, but he hoped for the kids' sake that Grey was wrong and they'd kept all their *special* gifts hidden away for later.

"Don't you start that," Gabby playfully scolded Grey and urged Daniel to open the gift. Cade stifled a laugh when the rosy blush on Daniel's cheeks bled into his ears and neck. After all they'd shared, public displays of affection, even between Gabby and her husbands, still made him uncomfortable.

Cade was always careful not to reach for his hand at family dinners, or allow his gaze to linger too long when they were anywhere but at home. For the most part, Cade was okay with their unspoken agreement, but he hoped one day Daniel would feel comfortable in his own skin, at least around his family—their family.

"Holy smokes!" Daniel whistled as he lifted the diamond honing stone from the box.

"It's the best knife sharpening stone they make," Mason said with a shrug. "I saw you struggling to get a good edge with that bench stone you bought from Burt's Hardware in town. That one there will put an edge so sharp on that fillet knife of yours, you'll have to watch you don't slice a finger off next time you're cleaning fish."

"You bet I will." Daniel tucked the stone back into its case and handed it to Cade to take a look. "Thanks, guys. I'll be sure to send a few fresh perch fillets your way when the stream thaws out."

Gabby's laugh captured everyone's attention as Grey's brother, Matt, shuffled his way into the new tandem baby sling Hazel had given them. While the family cooed over the newborn twins, Cade looked around the room and studied all their smiles, taking in the sheer joy of the holiday morning. They were an unusual lot to say the least: his sister and her three husbands, their three sons and Gabby, with their two sets of twins. He wouldn't trade a single one of them. Gabby and Daniel fit so seamlessly into the beautiful chaos; their places in the family tree seemed predestined.

"You're missing all the fun, son." His brother-in-law, Joe, clamped his hand over Grey's shoulder and reached for the video camera in his hand, recording the family's Christmas cheer. "Let me take the wheel a bit while you take a chunk out of that pile of presents."

"Joe, let him be," Hazel scolded her husband.

"Woman, I've been smelling that turkey all morning. All I'm saying is, let's move this party along."

"Opening the presents faster won't make the turkey cook any quicker, Josiah McLendon."

Cade glanced over at Hazel's other two husbands and burst out laughing. He couldn't help it. The 'we told you not to harass the cook' looks they gave Joe were priceless. His sister may be a tiny little thing, but she had their numbers, all three of them.

An hour or so later, they were buried in a mountain of discarded wrapping paper, glittery ribbons and shiny bows. Few gifts remained and Cade's insides began to twitch with anticipation. He checked the time on his wristwatch, ignoring Daniel's inquisitive glance, before turning his attention back to his eight-year-old grand-nephews, Connor and Carson, watching their eyes light up with excitement as Grey reached for the two big boxes tucked behind the tree.

"Last ones, boys."

"Yes!" Carson jumped to his feet and reached for the box in Grey's hands. Connor reached for the matching box and both boys tore into the paper with renewed excitement.

"Oh-My-Gosh!" Connor's mouth fell open as the picture on the box came into view. "Ohmygosh-ohmygosh-ohmygosh!" Connor bounced up and down as he tore open the top of the box and pulled out the new acoustic guitar, his mouth still gaping in shock.

"Awesome!" Carson shouted, pulling a shiny electric guitar from his box. "Holy moly! It's heavy!"

"Those come with a year's worth of lessons," Grey told them. "I don't want any excuses for missing them. Got it?"

"Oh man! We won't miss a single one!" Connor assured him. "Will we, Car?"

"No way!" Carson said. "We promise!" Both boys rushed Grey with excited hugs, repeating their declarations of gratitude with Gabby, Matt and Mason. "Can we go upstairs to play?"

"Give your Nanna and the Papas a hug and thank them, too," Gabby instructed. "Then take a load of your gifts upstairs first."

Cade's phone rang in his pocket, startling him out of the charming moment.

"Hello?" He handed Daniel the comic book his brother-in-law, Jake, had given him—a rare issue of Dr. Doom he needed to complete his collection—and hurried to excuse himself from the room, once again ignoring Daniel's questioning stare.

"We're here," Grant said on the other end of the line. "Where should I park? There's a half a dozen trucks parked along the driveway. I don't want to block anyone in."

Cade glanced over his shoulder to make sure no one had followed him from the room. "Park anywhere you want. I'm on my way out to meet you."

He shoved his feet into his boots and pushed his arms through the sleeves of his coat, his heart beating furiously with excitement. His gift to Daniel was here, and he couldn't wait to see the look on his face when he saw her.

Before he'd crossed the snow-covered distance between the house and Grant's car, the sound of a slamming door behind him stopped him in his tracks. He turned to see Grey barreling towards him, a fiery look in his eyes.

"Grey," he said, stepping in front of him, holding out his hand to slow his advance. "Let me explain."

Grey sidestepped him and stopped in front of the car, his hands on his hips, his unyielding gaze dancing between Grant and Natalie, who was still inside the car. "Is my family safe?" he asked Grant with a tone that insisted on nothing but the truth.

"I wouldn't have come if I didn't think—"

"You have a hell of a lot of enemies," he continued. "You positive about that?"

Grant paused and looked him in the eyes, tugging off his glove and reaching his hand out to Grey. "You have my word," he promised. "No one else knows we're here."

Cade held his breath as Grey studied Grant, releasing it with a huff as Grey reached out and shook Grant's hand, pulling him into an awkward hug. "Merry Christmas," Grey said, slapping Grant on the back. "Gabby and Daniel will be glad to see you."

When Grey retreated, Cade shook Grant's hand. "That part went better than I expected."

"Yeah, it did." Grant took a cursory glance around the ranch before he dipped his head and gave Natalie the all clear to get out of the car. "Let's hope the rest goes as smoothly."

"So," he nodded toward Natalie. "The two of you managed to make a go of it, huh?"

"Something like that," Grant said, offering no further details.

None were needed when he saw the way Grant hovered around her, holding her protectively in his embrace as they picked their way across the snow.

"Nice to see you again," Natalie said, ignoring Cade's outstretched hand, wrapping her arms around him instead. "I can't thank you enough for making this happen."

"Well, I…I can't take all the credit," he stammered, taken aback by her genuine smile and all of the other profound changes he saw. Daniel's daughter stood tall and proud, healthy, both inside and out, but most of all he noticed how her eyes met his with confidence. Gone was the lost and confused girl who'd struggled so profoundly to find her place in their lives. Standing before him was the strong woman they'd always hoped she'd become.

"Is he here?" she asked, nodding towards the house.

"Oh, yeah. Let's get you inside." He waived them on and led them through the snow and up the front steps. "I bet you haven't seen much snow," he said as he watched Grant show her how to kick the clumps off her boots.

Mimicking Grant, she kicked the edge of the top step with a little too much enthusiasm, laughing as the clumps of wet snow scattered across Grant's boots and jeans. "My first time, actually."

Cade opened the door and ushered them inside. "We'll have to make sure to do some sledding while you're here, then."

Voices of all different ages echoed down the hall as he led them to the family room where Daniel waited unaware. Cade's heart pounded against his chest and he said a silent prayer that he'd done the right thing. He knew he had, but he was bursting with so much anticipation it was impossible to contain it all with rational thought.

"Daniel! Gabby, babe," Grey said as he met them at the end of the hall. "I have someone here you might want to see."

Cade stepped aside and let Grant lead Natalie into the family room. A round of collective gasps preceded the sound of Daniel's voice.

"Grant?" Daniel moved the stack of gifts from his lap and stood. A kaleidoscope of emotions danced across his face: realization, confusion, hope, fear, and finally awe as Grant stepped aside and revealed Natalie's presence behind him.

"Nattie?" Daniel's eyes widened with disbelief.

No one in the room made a single sound or moved to greet them. Cade could barely breathe for the fullness in his chest. Daniel's gaze traveled from Natalie to him and back again. He loved Daniel so damn much in that moment.

"You did this?" he asked Cade, nodding to Thalia.

"I called him," Thalia confessed before he could answer. "I asked him not to tell you in case something happened and we couldn't make it."

Tears spilled over and ran unchecked down Daniel's cheeks. Cade lifted his hand and massaged the ache in his chest as Daniel turned his shocked gaze back to his daughter.

"Can I...uh...can I hug you?" Daniel asked with a wobbly voice, holding his arms wide with invitation.

Thalia's long legs ate up the distance between them as she crossed the room and sank into Daniel's anxious embrace. Two years of waiting. Cade fought back tears as he watched Daniel embrace his daughter for the first time since she'd left.

"Oh dear Lord, we're going to need more tissues." Hazel sniffled, swiping at her own tears.

It was then that he noticed Daniel's gift to Gabby had been opened in his brief absence. He studied it with regret that he'd missed seeing Gabby's reaction.

When they were on the run during her father's trial, Gabby lost the only picture she had of her late brother. When Daniel found out, he'd spent nights searching her father's case file until he found a surveillance photo of her brother they'd taken during the investigation. His nephews were excited to help Daniel, making a hand-carved frame for the enlargement. He'd hoped to see her open it, but judging by the teary eyes and abundance of tissues, it had been exactly the gift Daniel hoped it would be.

"I'll go see if I can find some tissues," Jake, Josiah, and Grey all said in unison and strode toward the kitchen.

"I need to go check on the turkeys," Hazel said. She snagged Gabby's hand and motioned for Matt and Mason to follow her. "Let's give them some privacy."

Cade paused in the doorway, giving them one last glance before he followed the rest of the family from the room. The way Daniel looked, so fulfilled and alive, with his daughter safely ensconced in his embrace was a sight that would stay with him for the rest of his life.

He was out in the barn with Hazel's husbands, helping feed the family's horses, when Daniel came looking for him.

"I think we're all done here," Joe said and motioned for his brother's to follow him outside.

Cade turned around to see Daniel standing at the end of the aisle beside the first stall door. Joe, Nate and Jake each gave Daniel a slap on the back as they filed out of the barn, leaving them to talk in private.

Dusting the hay from his hands, Cade walked over to Daniel, giving him a nervous wink. "I did well?"

Daniel reached out and pulled him into a crushing hug. "I love you," he said, his grip tightening to the point that he struggled to breathe. "I love you so damn much." Cade managed half a breath before Daniel took his face between his palms and kissed the living daylights out of him.

Yup, he'd done well. Any remnants of his fear of losing Daniel vanished as he embraced the man who'd been, and forever would be, the one true love of his life.

D.L. Roan

Chapter Fifteen

Present Day

A stray flurry landed on the windshield, pulling Cade from his memories. He shivered against the cold that had seeped inside the cab of his truck. Dying from hypothermia might be a better option than what he guessed he may be facing, but he wasn't ready to go just yet. He started the truck and drove the rest of the way down the long driveway, parking in front of his grand-nephews' house. He zipped up his coat before cutting the engine, opened the truck door and stepped out into the cold.

As he reached the top of the porch steps, the front door opened. "I was wondering how long you were going to sit out there," Carson greeted him.

His grand-nephews had grown to be upstanding young men, and country music superstars to boot. Those guitar lessons paid off big time, and now they lived on the ranch with their new wife, Breezy.

Winded from the rush to get out of the cold, he soaked in the warmth that greeted him when he stepped inside. "Looks like we're in for a nasty winter."

"Hey, Uncle Cade," Connor said, reaching out to pull him into a hug.

"What are you doing here?" Carson asked, offering to take his coat.

Cade waved him off. "I need to talk to Breezy. Is she here?"

"Yeah. She's upstairs," Connor said. "I'll go get her."

"Is everything okay?" Carson asked over his shoulder as Cade followed him deeper into the house to the main living room.

The house they'd built was nothing less than spectacular: heated tile floors, open rooms, tall ceilings, the latest appliances with all the trimmings of a Christmas turkey. When they'd first moved in, he'd hacked into all the smart appliances and played a few harmless pranks. No ice in the icemaker was fun. Auto-locking the washer was hysterical, especially when Carson did the laundry.

He'd never laughed so hard as when he ordered a dozen anchovy pizzas from their refrigerator, and piped seventies disco music into their internal audio system in the middle of the night, but they finally took him seriously about changing their default passwords and letting him install some extra security features. After the fiasco with the drones, when they'd first come back home, he'd have thought they would have been more careful.

"Is Daniel alright?"

"What?" He snapped his head up at Carson's question. "Oh, yeah. He's fine." Chilled to the bone, he took a seat in front of the roaring fire. "I need a few minutes of Breezy's time is all. Do you know if your mom ever heard from Jonah?"

"Hell no," Carson said. "I swear, when I get my hands on that kid, I'm going to kick his ass, after the dads get done with him."

Dammit. The thing with Jonah was such a damn mess. He didn't want to rat the kid out. He also didn't want to call him back home just because he may, or may not be, dying, but he wanted Jonah to make things right with the family. And, if things went as he suspected, he wanted to say goodbye while he still had his dignity.

"Hi, Uncle Cade," Breezy said with a warm smile as she descended the stairs and then gave a welcoming hug. Alongside Gabby and Daniel, Breezy was the best thing that had ever happened to their family. It took a special kind of woman to bring Con and Car to heel, but she did it effortlessly. "Con says you wanted to ask me about something. What's up?"

"I don't have a question, exactly," he said, looking past her to Con, and then to Car, hoping for some privacy.

"Oh," Con said awkwardly. "We have a vlog to record for the new single we're releasing next month, so...yeah. Car?"

As usual, it took Car a moment to catch on to the obvious. "Yeah, right. A vlog. We'll...let the two of you chat then." He gave Breezy a questioning glance before he and Con left the room.

"Is everything okay?" Breezy asked as soon as they were alone. "Is something wrong with Daniel?"

He shook his head. The words were on the tip of his tongue, but he couldn't get them past his lips.

"It's okay." Breezy laid her warm hand over his and gave it a comforting squeeze. "Whatever it is, let me help you."

Cade cleared his throat, crossed his legs, picked at a nonexistent piece of lint on his coat, all the fidgety, involuntary nervous ticks he'd long ago trained himself to resist, but couldn't seem to stop now. He looked at the doorway, and then back to Breezy, imagining himself apologizing for the misunderstanding and walking out. He couldn't. He couldn't drag this out any further and he needed her help.

"I'm pretty sure I'm dying," he finally blurted out, a vision of Daniel sitting beside him in the doctor's office, consumed with shock and grief, pushing the words from his mouth.

Breezy clutched her chest, tears pooling instantly in her eyes and streaming down her cheeks. He felt like a shit for springing it on her like that, but he didn't know how else to say it.

"What?" she asked, clearing the tears from her throat. "Dying of what?"

"I don't know yet," he said. "Some type of cancer I suppose."

"Wh—what do you mean, 'you don't know'?"

"We're waiting on the doctor to call back, but I think I already know what he's going to say. I'm old and tired." He shrugged and looked over at the flames licking at the logs in the fireplace. "I don't have all the official answers everyone will want to know, but that's why I'm here," he said, shifting in his seat as a sharp pain flared in his gut. "With your medical training, I'm sure you'll understand the doctor jargon a whole lot better than I will. Daniel's already a mess, and he'll be in no shape to remember anything they say. So, I was hoping you'd come with us to the doctor's office, to help make heads or tails of it all so we'll know what to tell the family."

Breezy's brows furrowed. She blinked back tears. "We knew you hadn't been feeling well, but what's happening? Is it the gallstones again?"

He nodded. "Probably a big part of it, but it's different this time. Something isn't right."

"Are you in pain?" she asked, her gaze roaming his body, stopping on the hand he pressed against the gripping pain.

"It's bearable, for now." He released his side and shifted in his seat, the pain subsiding a bit with the new position. "Will you come with us? To the doctor's?"

"Of course I will but, Uncle Cade, even if it is cancer—and there's a thousand other things it could be—they have new treatments now, new medications. They can do a lot to—"

"I'm not doing any of that," he assured her, unwilling to allow her or anyone else to entertain false hope. "I've lived a good life for near seventy years and, well, dying is part of the bargain, I guess. I won't spend my last days in and out of doctors' offices, puking my guts up and losing what dignity I have left just to eke out a few extra months."

"Oh, Cade." Breezy slid from her seat and crouched at his feet, holding his hand to her cheek. "I'll do whatever I can to help you, you know that, but please promise me you'll at least consider what the doctors say."

"I promise I'll hear them out, but that's all," he insisted. "I'm sorry I dumped all of this on you, but I'd appreciate you being there. Daniel will need you more than I will, I figure."

"I'll be there every step of the way, whatever they find." Breezy promised. "Have you discussed any of this with Daniel?"

Cade shook his head. "You're the only one I've told. I don't want him or the family getting all twisted up about it until we know what we're dealing with."

Breezy nodded and stood, wiping away her tears. "I guess I'd better turn off the waterworks, then. Con and Car will spit kittens if they see I've been crying."

He chuckled. "They learned that from their fathers." Spitting kittens was an acquired skill, and a damn fascinating one at that. "You can tell them if they ask, but please make sure they keep their traps shut until after the appointment."

"I will," Breezy sighed. "Don't worry."

"I'd like to tell everyone at the same time, you know? Rip the bandage off all at once so we can move on to whatever comes next."

"When's the doctor supposed to call?"

He walked beside her as they turned for the front door, lamenting the loss of the warmth of their hearth. "It's Saturday night, so, with doctor's hours and such, I imagine it will be Monday before we hear anything."

"When did you have the tests done?"

"Yesterday," he said. "They did so many scans and tests I expected to glow in the dark when we went to bed last night."

"Well," Breezy said with a strained laugh, "if they do find something serious they won't wait. Slow news is good news."

He managed a smile. It was human nature to want to believe in a more favorable outcome, no matter what the odds against it.

"Thank you," Cade said and gave her one last hug. "Just knowing you'll be there helps more than you know."

"It's no problem at all." She leaned in and gave him a kiss on the cheek. "I know it's pointless to say, but please try not to worry too much. I hope it's something simple, but whatever happens, you know we'll be there for you, and for Daniel."

The road passed beneath his truck like a lazy river on the drive back home. He drove slowly, stretching out the short trip to search for a way to tell Daniel what he feared was his inevitable fate. He still didn't know where to begin by the time he reached their driveway and his cellphone rang beside him.

The sun had set and the light on the screen lit up the cab of his truck like a warning beacon. He looked down at the screen and noted the unfamiliar number. If slow news was good news, it must be worse than he thought. Despite being chilled to the bone, sweat laced his palms as he reached over and swiped the screen to answer it.

"Hello?"

"Uncle Cade?"

"Jonah?" He slumped back in the driver's seat as his last breath rushed from his lungs. "What in hell have you been doing? Do you have any idea how many emails Papa Daniel has sent you?"

"I know," Jonah sighed. "I just spoke to him. He said you're sick. What's wrong?"

Cade closed his eyes and pinched the bridge of his nose. He should have known Daniel would rat him out. "Nothing you need to worry about, but if you don't get home soon, we're blowing your cover. Your mom is making herself sick worrying about you."

Jonah was quiet for a long time before a string of muffled curses bled through the static in their connection. "Shit. I have to go, but I'll be home soon," he finally said. "I'm sorry I lied to you, but please don't tell mom and the dads where I am. I'll tell them everything when I get there."

"You'd better," Cade warned.

"I will. I promise."

"Don't drag your feet. And don't tell your parents about me being sick if you talk to them!" he added. The last thing he needed was a flood of McLendons at his front door, demanding answers he didn't yet have.

"I won't. I'm sorry, Uncle Cade. I gotta go."

He let the phone drop after the call abruptly ended. "Fool-hearted kid." Had he ever been so careless with his loved ones? He knew the answer before he'd even finished the thought, cursing the ignorance of youth as he unbuckled his seatbelt and slid out of the truck.

Snow fell heavily now and clumped in his hair as he made his way up the steps to the front door. *At least I have that going for me*, he thought as his knees crackled with each step. He would die with all his teeth, a full head of hair and having known the love of a good man. *A good man with a big mouth.*

The aroma of garlic and homemade tomato sauce breathed fresh life into his waning appetite as he stepped through the front door and kicked off his boots.

"Jonah called." The sound of Daniel's voice preceded his appearance in the hallway.

"I spoke to him," Cade said and peeled off his jacket.

"Shit." Daniel sighed and pinched the back of his neck, a contrite expression on his face as he stared at the cracks in the hardwood floor. "I asked him not to call you."

"Asking a lot from a kid who's running from his own shadow."

Daniel shrugged. "He was hedging. Guilt is his Achilles heel."

"Did you tell anyone else? The Associated Press, maybe?"

"That's not fair," Daniel argued. "And who's he going to tell? It took an act of congress to get him to return a damn phone call."

Cade pushed past him into the kitchen and rummaged through the refrigerator for a beer. When he didn't find one, he slammed the door and opted for a glass of water instead. "I didn't want anyone to know until we heard back from the doctor."

"Then you should have said something."

"I figured it was obvious. I haven't even told you."

The second the words left his mouth he wanted to kick himself. The look of confused fear on Daniel's face was enough to make him wish he'd gagged them back. Daniel didn't need or deserve the fight he was picking.

"Haven't told me what? Did the doctor call?"

Cade shook his head. "No. And I don't know what the hell I'm saying, so just forget it."

He took a seat at the kitchen table, all set with plates and glasses and all the fixings for a tasty spaghetti dinner he no longer had the appetite to eat. "Looks good," he said anyway and scooped up a plateful of noodles. "What?" he asked when Daniel remained standing in the kitchen doorway, staring at him with those damn eyes that looked too hard for the things he could no longer hide.

"You think I'm stupid."

"What? No."

"You must think I'm a complete moron."

Cade closed his eyes and took a deep breath. "I do not think—"

"You think I don't see it? That I don't notice every single pound you've lost? Every cautious step you take up those steps, or that you're out of breath by the time you get to the top? You think I don't see the bags under your eyes from being so damn exhausted you should sleep for a week, but can't because the pain keeps you awake every night? Or every time you mask the pain with that damn expressionless look you think hides the real you from the rest of the world? Well, fuck you. I see it all!"

"Why are you so angry?"

"I'm not angry. I'm scared as hell!"

Cade's fork clanged against his plate and tumbled to the floor as he pushed from the table and walked over to his lover. He reached up and gripped Daniel's neck, pulling him close until they were forehead to forehead.

"Don't be scared," he whispered.

"I *am* scared," Daniel whispered back. "It's not enough time."

He pressed his lips to Daniel's, knowing it wouldn't be enough to change anything. "There'll never be enough time."

Daniel's rigid spine softened and Cade gathered him into his arms. His chest rose and fell with his anxious breaths and Cade leaned into it, listening to the frantic rhythm of his heart. When the beat slowed, he lifted his head and glanced up at Daniel. "I didn't mean to snap at you. And I didn't mean to shut you out."

"I don't understand why you wouldn't tell me."

"Because of this," he insisted. "You obsess about things and I knew you'd get all bent out of shape."

"I don't obsess."

Cade sighed. "You're worse than Hazel when it comes to being an old mothering hen."

"I am *not* an old mothering hen."

"You are," he insisted.

Daniel looked like he would argue, but didn't. He knew Cade was right. "I didn't want you to worry until we know for sure there's something to worry about."

"But you think there is."

Cade looked away, but nodded. Admitting aloud to Daniel what he suspected was physically impossible, but maybe he'd been wrong to shut him out completely.

Daniel was a man's man, both inside and out, but deep down in the very core of who he was, existed an emotional creature that needed to nurture and protect the ones he loved. That gooey center was Cade's Achilles heel, what he loved most about him, and he needed to remind himself of that from time to time.

He took Daniel by the hand, pressing a finger to his lips when he tried to say more, and led him up the stairs. Their bedroom was dark but warm, the way they both liked it, as he folded back the covers. Not bothering to undress, he slid to the middle of the bed and tugged Daniel into his arms. "I need you to hold me for a while," Cade said as he tucked the covers around them and lost himself in the familiarity of his lover's warm body.

Dinner could wait. Talking could wait. Dying could wait.

Daniel released a helpless whimper as he snuggled closer. "I'm not ready for this."

He nuzzled the side of Daniel's neck, inhaling the lingering scent of his aftershave, and something that smelled suspiciously like pain relief cream.

Neither am I.

Chapter Sixteen

Daniel sat in the waiting room, Cade on his left, Breezy on his right, and counted the ceiling tiles for the umpteenth time. His stomach was still in knots from breakfast, when the scheduling nurse called and asked them to come in. Any speculation or hope that Cade was simply having another gallstone attack was extinguished, a new kind of hell springing up in its place. Doctors didn't dish out bad news over the phone.

Every time the door to the waiting room opened and the nurse came out with a file in her hand, another wave of angst flooded Daniel's veins and caused him to break out into a fresh sweat. By the time his heart rate returned to a non-lethal level, the door would swing open again and she'd call another patient's name.

He was going out of his mind one patient at a time.

Having counted forward, backward and diagonally, he forced his gaze from the ceiling and glanced over at Cade, amazed at the level of calm and strength he exuded. Relaxed in the uncomfortable chair, his weathered hands crossed over his lap, his expression blank, as if he was waiting for something as trivial as his number to be called at the supermarket deli counter.

Daniel stiffened his spine and sucked in a fortifying breath. If Cade could do this, so could he. He had to. Cade had been his rock during the most terrifying times in his life. He needed to man up and return that strength, do the hard things. He owed Cade that and so much more.

The front door swung open and two more patients walked in. He looked up and was surprised to see their neighbor, Dirk Grunion, and his wife enter the waiting room. Breezy stiffened beside him as they walked inside, Dirk giving them a hardened stare before they continued to the check-in counter.

He reached over and took Breezy's hand. The long-running feud between the Grunions and the McLendons had ratcheted up to historic levels in recent years. He didn't know the details of the latest skirmish, but he'd put enough pieces together to know Breezy had accumulated a few battle scars of her own since marrying Connor and Carson.

"I have a two o'clock with Dr. Fielding," he overheard Dirk say in his usual gruff tone.

He couldn't help but notice the amount of weight Dirk had gained since the last time their paths crossed. The puffiness in his skin seemed more ominous than a few too many cheeseburgers.

His wife led him to a duet of chairs on the other side of the waiting room—the farthest away from them, he noted with a smirk. Dirk reached down and opened up a magazine, pretending to be immediately engrossed in whatever was on the pages, but Daniel didn't miss the way the middle-aged man struggled to catch his breath.

He didn't know how sick Dirk was, but he hoped for his son's sake it wasn't too serious. Despite their differences, Pryce Grunion was a good kid, much too young to lose his father, even if Dirk was an ass.

"Cade Candelle," the nurse said as the door swung open once again.

Halle-fucking-lujah!

Cade rose with a confident nod and Daniel followed him down the hall into a small conference room, his mouth suddenly so dry he didn't dare try to swallow.

This is it.

For the last hour he'd sat in the waiting room, anxious to get this over with, but now he felt as if he were being marched in front of a firing squad, and wished for more time.

Breezy laid a comforting hand on his shoulder, reminding him of her presence as they waited for the nurse to retrieve an extra seat for her.

"Go ahead, please," he choked out and motioned for her to take the seat beside Cade, but she refused, insisting she'd wait. He was embarrassingly grateful as he sank down into the upholstered chair before he passed out beside it.

Get yourself together! Cade needs you. Unaware of when they'd entered the room, Daniel repeated the silent mantra in his head until Dr. Hillsborough and an older doctor he didn't recognize appeared.

"Cade, Daniel," Dr. Hillsborough shook their hands. "I'm sorry, but I'm not sure we've met," he said when he got to Breezy.

"That's my grand-niece, Breezy McLendon," Cade said. "I asked her to come because she has some medical training. I figure she'll know the right questions to ask about whatever news you have for us."

"Are you a doctor?" he asked.

"Occupational therapist," Breezy replied.

"Oh! You're the McLendon Twins' wife, right? I'm a huge fan of your husbands' songs."

"Thank you," Breezy said with a tense smile as the doctor gave her hand an enthusiastic shake.

Daniel stiffened in his seat, the doctor's cavalier manner grating on his nerves. Ripping someone's family apart shouldn't be so exciting. Cade sensed his agitation and placed a calming hand on his bouncing knee.

"Cade, this is Dr. Lector," Dr. Hillsborough introduced the man beside him.

The blood drained from Daniel's face. "You're joking, right?"

"Your first name isn't Hannibal is it?" Cade asked with a forced smile as he shook the doctor's hand.

"Victor," the older doctor said with a knowing smile. "It's Lector with an 'O', so no need to worry."

Daniel couldn't believe what he was hearing. "Victor? As in Victor Von Doom?"

"Holy shit. I didn't even catch that one," Cade said with a chuckle. "You should wear a green coat."

Dr. Lector grinned as he acknowledged the reference to the popular comic book character. "I haven't thought about it, to be honest. I'll have to look into that."

Daniel didn't like the odd mixture of emotions their conversation stirred. He knew Cade's way of dealing with shitty situations was to turn everything into a joke, and on any other day he would laugh with him, but in the face of losing the love of his life he couldn't quite grasp the comedic relief of the moment.

"Cade, I've asked Dr. Lector to join us today because he's an oncologist and specializes in the type of treatment you'll need for your condition." Dr. Hillsborough's interruption dispelled the light-hearted mood in the room.

Breezy gasped beside him, her quiet sob confirming he wasn't trapped inside a nightmare, but living one.

Oncologist. The knots in his stomach twisted tighter.

"So I have cancer?" Cade asked after clearing his throat, his eyes narrowing to slits as he braced for the confirmation.

"It's never easy to say this, but yes," Dr. Lector said with a sympathetic nod. He could see the way the man struggled as he prepared to tell them the rest of the awful news. Daniel felt a moment's pity for the guy before he opened the file in his hands and gave it to them with both barrels. "I'm sorry to have to tell you this, but you have pancreatic cancer."

The word *cancer* hit Daniel square in the chest, knocking the wind out of him. His hands tightened in a white-knuckled grip around the armrests on his chair as he absorbed the blow. *Cade has cancer.* He'd gone in knowing it was possible, but this...this didn't seem real. *Is this really happening?*

He closed his eyes and resisted the urge to shout at the top of his lungs how unfair it was. Cade pried his fingers from the chair and took hold of his hand, but the effort was useless. Daniel's mind went blank. Everything compressed into one singular task; keeping his shit together in front of Cade. *I will not cry,* he repeated in his head, over and over as the doctor continued to speak. He blinked away the sting in his eyes and swallowed, but the lack of saliva in his mouth made his tongue stick to the back of his throat.

Breezy patted him on the back as he coughed and tried to clear his throat, but the sting persisted.

"Here, drink this." He took the cupful of water from Dr. Doom's hand and tossed it back, wadding the paper cup in his fist as he cleared his throat and sat back in his seat. Cade took his hand again and, just like that, they were back on the firing line, facing another round of fatal wounds.

"Based on the enzyme markers in your blood tests, I'm going to stage your cancer at two, but with the size of the tumor on your pancreas, I'm more inclined to believe you're closer to stage three."

Stage three. Stage three. What does that mean?

"I won't know for sure until I can see if the cancer cells have spread into the adjacent organs or large blood vessels, but I'll need to run some more tests to know that."

"So, if it hasn't spread you can operate, right?" Daniel asked, grasping onto every hair-thin thread he could find in what Dr. Doom was saying.

"We need to operate regardless," Dr. Hillsborough said, jerking the thread from his grasp. "That's where I come in."

"What do you mean?" Cade asked, his grip tightening around his hand. "Why have my gallbladder taken out when I'm going to die anyway?"

Dr. Hillsborough clicked a button on the open laptop in front of him, and an x-ray photo of Cade's abdomen appeared on the television screen hanging behind him. "Not all of the pain you're experiencing is caused by the cancer." He took a pointer and circled a clump of white dots on the screen. "You have a cluster of gallstones here." He moved over to the right an inch and circled another white dot. "But this one is blocking the bile duct in your pancreas, causing most of your pain and explains the vomiting and sudden loss of appetite."

"Is that what caused the cancer?" Breezy asked.

Dr. Doom shook his head. "It's one of those chicken or egg questions," he said. "It's possible, though there were no traces of the tumor when the previous gallstones were removed. The new stone could have been encapsulated by the tumor as it grew. We'll never know, but it's why I'll need to be present during the removal of the stones. I can remove whatever amount of the tumor may be blocking the ducts and put in stints to keep them open, which will keep them from clogging and make palliative care a lot easier through the later stages."

"Palliative care?" Cade asked.

"Mr. Candelle, I'm going to be honest. I'm not optimistic about removing your tumor," Dr. Doom continued. "Even if it's an option, the survival rate for this type of cancer beyond any considerable length of time is very low for someone of your age, even with chemotherapy and radiation. The most we're probably going to be able to do for you, other than remove the blockage, will be to further ease your pain and make you as comfortable as possible."

The air rushed from Cade's lungs and Daniel wiped the wetness from his eyes. He wasn't supposed to cry, dammit!

"Is chemo or radiation even an option?" Breezy asked with an unsteady voice that made it all that much harder to hold back his own tears.

"I already told you I'm not doing any of that," Cade insisted, the calm resignation in his voice confirming to Daniel that he'd already accepted his fate.

Breezy plucked a handful of tissues from the box in the middle of the table, her tears falling unrestrained. Cade reached across his lap and took Breezy's hand as she cried.

"I'm sorry," she said between sniffles. "I'm supposed to be here to help you."

"You are helping." He patted her hand. "You're doing fine."

Daniel felt like such a helpless ass. Cade was the one dying and he was just sitting there, dumbfounded, incapable of doing anything more than breathing, and a piss poor job of it at that. His world was falling apart at the seams, but he couldn't let Cade down. He swallowed hard, managing not to choke this time, and sat stiffly against the back of the chair.

"How—" The words stuck in his dry throat, but he dragged in a shaky breath and tried again. "How long?"

"On the optimistic side? A year." Dr. Doom's voice droned on with what he suspected was a standard spiel. "Maybe a couple of months longer with chemo and radiation. On the conservative side, and more realistic, you're looking at eight to ten months."

Eight to ten months. Eight to ten months. Eight to ten months.

The words spun around in his head, over and over, drowning out everything else until the room began to close in on him and he couldn't sit there another second.

"I need to go to the restroom," he said and bolted from the chair. His knees popped with the sudden movement, but he didn't feel the pain that typically accompanied the crunching sound. "Will you be alright?" he forced himself to turn around and ask Cade before he ran out of the room with his tail tucked between his legs, praying he said yes because he was about to lose his breakfast in the middle of the conference room.

"We'll be fine," Breezy assured him with a wobbly smile. "Are you okay? You look pale."

He couldn't answer her. He spun on his heels and rushed from the room. The narrow hallways shrank even more as he wandered through the maze of doors and windows looking for the men's room, opting for the back door when he didn't find one.

The frigid air outside stung his lungs, but relief didn't come quick enough to calm the storm brewing inside. He stumbled into the snow and hunched over, decorating a nearby barren shrub with the contents of his stomach.

"Sir, are you alright?" A nurse called from the doorway he'd propelled himself through.

He held up a staying hand and gave her a nod, but she didn't leave. "I'm fine," he said, but he wasn't.

Cade was dying.

D.L. Roan

Chapter Seventeen

Daniel stared out the passenger window at the snow-covered fields, each one blurring into the next as they drove by on their way home. The warmth of Cade's hand bled into his palm, but the frigid landscape held his thoughts captive. How had this happened? Where did all the time go?

It seemed like only yesterday he was standing in the airport in Germany, agitated and alone, with no plans for his future. Even the word 'future' seemed like some far-off fantasy that only existed in the context of theory and speculation. Somewhere along the line he blinked and that theoretical world became reality. He was afraid to blink again, should it all disappear into the dustbin of history.

"Papa Daniel."

The sound of Breezy's voice interrupted his melancholic thoughts. He blinked, finding himself sitting in the truck in front of their house. Glancing back at Breezy, he thought about the day he met her, the day her brother died and he held the broken teenaged-version of her in his arms as she grieved. Then he remembered the day she married Connor and Carson. It was the first time he'd realized how quickly time had passed.

The heat of Cade's touch disappeared and he glanced down at his empty hand. *Just like that*, he thought, as he watched Cade circle the truck and open his door. Life had passed them by, and soon Cade would be gone, too.

"I'll have Con and Car drive the truck back over when they get home from the studio, okay?"

"Sure." He nodded and reached for her hand before he got out. "Thank you," he said, regretting his disconnected tone. "For everything." She'd been a godsend—taking notes, asking questions, setting up the appointments for the tests Cade needed. He would have to call her later, after he'd pulled himself together, and find out what they had to do next.

"Love you," she said as he closed the door and followed Cade up onto the porch, watching her weave her way back down the driveway.

"I'm glad she came," he said as the tail lights blinked one final time and she pulled onto the road, once again amazed Cade had had the forethought to ask her.

"Me too," Cade said and opened the door.

The house was eerily quiet as they toed off their boots and hung their coats. He followed Cade into the kitchen, watched as he took two glasses from the cupboard and filled them with water. Daniel committed the scene to memory as Cade twisted the cap off the ibuprofen. The sound of the pills rattling in the bottle as he shook some out was harsh against the quietness.

The water trembled in the glasses as Cade crossed the kitchen. He placed two tablets in the palm of Daniel's hand and then handed him one of the glasses before he swallowed his own pills.

Daniel stared at the pills, his thoughts jumbled, his body numb. "I don't know what to do," he admitted. He was so lost. He wanted to be strong, but he was failing miserably. He should be the one trying to make Cade comfortable.

"Take the pills," Cade instructed.

He stared at the pills, the simple task requiring deliberate thought before he tossed them to the back of his throat and washed them down with a gulp of water.

Cade took the glass from him and set it on the kitchen counter with his own. Daniel watched him, feeling the need to chronicle his every move, every second that remained of their time together.

When Cade reached up and cupped the sides of his neck, he tried to look at him, but the numbers kept running through his head. *Eight to ten months.* Cade would never see another Christmas. He pressed his lips together, held his breath, swallowed, but nothing could hold back the sob that broke from the painful knot in his chest.

"Shh." Cade pressed their foreheads together. "Don't cry for me. Don't cry for us." Cade rarely revealed his emotions, but Daniel caught the glassy look in his eyes as he swiped away his own tears with the pads of his thumbs. "We've had our happily ever after. Lived it to the fullest." He firmed his grip and Daniel met his eyes. "Don't you get it? I've seen and done everything I've ever wanted, and I got to do it all with you. There's nothing left for me to do except wait for you on the other side."

Daniel nodded, unable to speak, his tears still choking his throat. They stood together in the middle of the kitchen, surrounded once again by the silence, as he soaked up the feel of Cade in his arms. Cade was right. He would have to let him go, and damn it hurt. It hurt worse than anything he could have imagined.

Cade leaned in and pressed his lips to Daniel's. The kiss wasn't seductive or sensual, but borne of friendship and love, practiced and perfected over decades of intimate comfort.

"Hey," Cade said, lifting his head. "At least it's not prostate cancer, or testicular cancer." He grinned as he reached down and cupped his groin. "I'm going down with all the important bits intact."

Daniel fought back a grin as he turned away and scrubbed his hands over his face to dispel his tears. "How can you joke at a time like this?"

Cade laughed. "How can I not? Seriously. Can you imagine me with one old man ball, swinging to and fro?" He swiveled his hips in a circle and Daniel snorted.

"Stop, please." He squeezed his eyes closed to block out the image and leaned his forehead against Cade's once again. Cade gave his hips one last twist and Daniel shook his head. "You're impossible."

They laughed together, but Daniel's heart still ached as acceptance took root. Cade was leaving him, and there wasn't a damn thing he could do about it. He needed to pull himself together so he could be there when Cade needed him most, but where did he start? "I still don't know what to do."

"We do the same thing we've always done, until we can't," Cade replied. "We take one day at a time and deal with things as they come."

Daniel nodded, because nodding was easier than speaking. That sounded doable. *One day at a time.*

Cade's fingers tightened on his forearms. Alarm coursed through Daniel when Cade backed away from his embrace and walked across the kitchen, bracing against the sink.

"What's wrong?"

Cade didn't answer him, flipping on the faucet and splashing a handful of water on his face instead.

"You have to be honest with me," Daniel insisted, handing him a clean dish towel.

Cade dried his face and hands and finally turned to face him. Daniel gasped when he saw his pallid expression. That damn mask he hid behind was gone, revealing for the first time how truly sick he was. The pain, the weakness, the exhaustion were all laid bare before him, undiluted by any attempt to hide them. It took his breath away.

Daniels grief turned to anger. How dare Cade keep this from him? How dare he shoulder it all alone and take away his right—his need—to help? He wanted to shout the words, to shove Cade against the counter and demand answers he wouldn't accept, but he couldn't do any of those things. Not now.

"You can't lie to me anymore," he insisted, tempering his words with as much restraint as he could muster. He pulled out a seat at the kitchen table and guided Cade to sit while he filled another glass full of water. "I'm a mess right now. I'm going to be sad and angry and worry, but I'm not a child you need to protect from the truth. I can—I will—be there for you. But that only works if you let me."

"It's just nausea. It'll go away."

"I don't care if it's a goddamn pimple on your ass," he said as he set the glass in front of him on the table and sank down in the other chair. "I want to know about it!"

Cade raised his brow, glaring at him incredulously over the rim of his glass as he took several careful sips.

"Okay, maybe not that much information, but you know what I mean."

Cade set the glass down and gave him a nod. "I'll tell you if I need something I can't—or don't feel well enough to do for myself," he added when Daniel gave him a challenging stare.

"And if you're sick, you go to the doctor. No questions asked."

"I'll go if I need to, but not for every hiccup or 'ass pimple'," he challenged. "I'm not going to spend what time I have left paying the doctors' golf club fees."

"Fine," Daniel capitulated. "But you're having the surgery." Though it was pointless to bring it up now, he suspected Cade's phobia of being sedated, and doctors in general, had allowed the tumor to grow unchecked in the first place. Despite what the doctor said, he couldn't help but think that, if he'd gone back when he first suspected the gallstones had returned, he might have caught the cancer in time. Now they would never know.

Cade opened his mouth to argue, but closed it with a sigh and a nod. "If it will get the most out of what's left of me, I'll have the surgery."

They sat quietly and waited for the nausea to pass. There were a thousand more things he wanted to say, questions he had, but lacked the fortitude to ask. He was tired. Cade was exhausted. He'd hovered enough for one day, but he couldn't help but ask, "Is there anything else I can do for you?"

Cade gave him a salacious grin and Daniel rolled his eyes. They both laughed, but Cade soon sobered, his fingers drawing lines in the condensation gathered on his glass of water. "Do you remember the first day we met?"

"Yes." How could he forget?

"I knew we would have an affair," Cade admitted, his lips turning up into his lazy grin Daniel loved so much, "but I also knew there would be more, that we had a story to live."

Daniel rested his arms on the table and leaned against the back of his chair as he remembered that day. "I just wanted your ass."

Cade chuckled. "I'd never met a man so captivated by my ass." They laughed again, but Cade continued. "I said earlier that I've lived a good life, and I meant it. We've lived our story, and it was a good one, but I don't want it to end with sadness and all this gloom. I want to go out with no regrets, celebrating us and our story."

Daniel tensed in his seat. He'd do anything Cade asked him to, but he hoped like hell he was hearing him wrong. "Are you asking what I think you're asking?"

"I'm saying that I want to make our last chapter the best chapter," Cade said, and glanced up at Daniel, holding his gaze. "Will you help me do that?"

Daniel blew out a relieved breath and slid his hand over Cade's. "Yes," he said and meant it, but he couldn't deny his relief. "Jesus. I thought for a second there, you were going to ask me to marry you."

"Do you want to get married?" Cade asked, his tone sober, his expression again unreadable. "Gay marriage is legal now."

Daniel froze, his heart rate increasing to induce an instant sweaty sheen on his palms. "Do *you* want to get married?"

He would if Cade asked, without complaint, but his last disastrous marriage aside, he wasn't sure he'd ever be ready to make such a public declaration. He'd tried to protect Natalie from that part of himself when she was a child. The world was different back then, but he'd never been ashamed of Cade, or the life they'd built since. He understood the world had changed—for the most part—and the stigmas associated with homosexual relationships had changed with it, but his deep-seated need to hold that part of himself close had never caught up with the times. He'd never once felt their relationship had suffered from the lack of a piece of paper with a bunch of official signatures on it. Maybe Cade had.

"I wish you could see the terrified look on your face," Cade said with a cunning grin. Before Daniel could utter the string of curses running through his head, Cade reached for his hand and tugged him to his feet. "I've always loved being able to read your thoughts, especially when you're scrambling to dodge a question."

"I'm not dodging," he insisted, "or scrambling. I haven't thought much about—"

"I don't want to get married unless we need to for all the legal stuff," Cade interrupted his rambling, putting him out of his misery. "But I wouldn't mind a honeymoon."

"A honeymoon?"

"Mmm-hmm," Cade nodded and draped his arms over Daniel's shoulders. "If, after the surgery, I'm feeling better, let's take a road trip somewhere, just you and me."

"A road trip?" Would that be wise? He didn't like the idea of putting that kind of distance between Cade and his doctors.

"Come on," Cade urged. "We can even rent that RV you've been trying to talk me into buying for the last decade. Drive the countryside like we used to in Germany. Our first stop can be one of those dispensaries in Colorado. Pick us up some of that good shit."

"You want to go buy pot?"

"Why not?" Cade shrugged. "Might as well. Fuck it. I'll go down tomorrow and sign up for one of those medical marijuana cards. In fact," he said with another shrug, some of the tension falling from his shoulders, "I'm going to make a whole damn fuck-it list."

"A what list?"

"A fuck-it list," he laughed. "You know, instead of a bucket list. I'm going to make a list of all the things I don't have time to give a fuck about anymore, like smoking weed. Who the hell cares? And wearing underwear. I'm done with that."

Cade was so serious Daniel couldn't help but laugh. "We'll make a bonfire and burn every pair of tighty-whities in the house. And if anyone asks about the bulge in your jeans, down by your knee, we'll just tell'em it's your one old man ball."

"Fuck you," Cade said with a grin. "Are we doing this, or not?"

"Yeah." Daniel nodded with a reluctant sigh. "We'll do it, but only if you're feeling better after the surgery."

"Deal."

Daniel hugged his lover close, incapable of refusing him anything. They could take a hundred road trips, have a thousand honeymoons, it still wouldn't be enough. He'd never been a religious man, but hidden away in a secret place inside his heart was hope that Cade was right. He prayed they'd find each other again on the other side of death. But even if they did, he knew deep down in that same secret place, this would be their hardest goodbye.

Chapter Eighteen

The waiting room at the outpatient center seemed crowded for such an early hour. The first morning rays of sun were racing across the sky, shining through the large glass windows and landing on Daniel's back, thawing some of the late January chill from his bones.

Cade's tests had revealed the cancer hadn't spread beyond the tumor, but the operation required to remove it was risky at best and offered no guarantees. As much as it hurt, he supported Cade's decision to stick with the original plan—to only remove the blockage and put in any necessary stints. The procedure was a simple one, not much more complicated than the one he'd had before, but Cade was still a walking wreck.

He'd woken an hour before their alarm was set to go off and took a walk in the fields beside their house. Daniel let him go, watching him from the bedroom window. He didn't know if he was praying or just thinking, but Daniel had felt the urge to say a prayer anyway.

If all went well today, Cade could expect to feel better before he began to feel worse again. Daniel had prayed all morning for that to be true. Now there was nothing left to do but wait.

There was an endless stream of patients and nurses coming and going. Ringing phones went unanswered. The entire room was abuzz with constant distraction, but Cade didn't miss the hungry roar of Daniel's stomach.

"Oh for Christ's sake, go get something to eat," Cade grumbled beside him.

Daniel shook his head. Out of respect for Cade's mandatory fasting instructions, he'd skipped breakfast and their morning coffee. "You know the second I leave they'll call you back."

"So," Cade said with a smirk. "You don't have to babysit me. I'm not going AWOL."

The corners of Daniel's lips curled up as he imagined Cade sneaking down the hall in a hospital gown, one hand clutching a rolling IV stand, the other the open back of his gown to hide his bare ass as he tried to make a break for it.

"You sure about that?" he asked. Cade looked away and he laughed. "That's what I thought."

"I'll go get you something," Gabby offered from where she and Grey sat across from them.

Once all the tests were done and the surgery was scheduled, they'd held a family meeting—Jonah excluded. The sulking kid had reverted back to ignoring their calls and emails. If he wasn't home by the time he and Cade were, he'd resolved to tell Gabby and his dads everything. As his dad Matt would say, if Jonah was old enough to be a fuckwad, then he was old enough to deal with the consequences.

Expectedly, the news of Cade's cancer hit them all hard. There were countless tears of course, a good bit of them from Hazel and Gabby, but Dani had broken his heart with her sobs. It was her first brush with loss. Something he knew all too well. They might not be genetically related, but she was a lot like him. She loved with her whole heart, and losing Cade would be like losing a piece of herself. He hoped he would be around to see her find the kind of love he and Cade had, but even if he wasn't, he knew that the man who captured her heart would have it forever.

"If they call you before I get back, I'll eat whatever I find. I'm starving," Gabby shouldered her purse.

"I'll be fine," he insisted, his last word cut off with a wide yawn. "But you can go ahead if you're hungry."

"Nonsense," Gabby insisted. "At least let me go get you a fresh coffee."

"Great idea. I'll go," Grey offered with a sour expression. "The swill they're serving at the nurse's station tastes like something from the fertilizer shed."

He grinned at Gabby as Grey disappeared around the corner as quick as he could get to his feet. "He still hates hospitals, huh?"

Gabby rolled her eyes and nodded. "Almost as much as he hates my new car."

"*I* hate you're new car," Cade said with a grunt. "Can't believe you went back to driving a go-kart."

"She's *not* a go-kart, or a golf cart, or any of the other horrible insults all of you hurl at her," Gabby insisted. "Since the guys insist on driving if there's even so much as a chance of snow, I see no point in having my own behemoth truck when they have three to choose from. And besides, I've always wanted a convertible."

"Which will be sitting useless in the equipment barn until at least May," Cade scoffed.

"Cade Candelle?" A boisterous voice called from the nurse's station.

"What'd I tell you," Daniel griped as he stood. "As soon as someone leaves…"

"It's like they have a camera trained on your every move," Cade muttered beside Daniel as he stood slowly, wincing with the effort. "The second they know your reinforcements are gone, they send in the troops."

"Love you," Gabby said as she hugged first him and then Cade. "We'll be here when you wake up."

"I'll be back as soon as they wheel him into the operating room," Daniel told her.

The nurse led them through the double doors into the bowels of the surgery center. One turn led to another, each hallway identical to the next until they reached a central staging area and they were led into a small room with a gurney and a single chair.

Everything from that point on was hurry up and wait. Nurses came and went, each one taking Cade's vitals and writing in his chart.

Stripped down to his birthday suit, Cade handed over his clothes and shoes. Daniel placed them in a plastic bag and took a seat while Cade donned the pink and yellow checkered hospital gown.

"Cute," he teased as Cade slid onto the gurney. "Pink is your color."

"Fuck you," was his only reply.

More minutes passed and Cade became uncharacteristically restless, crossing and uncrossing his ankles, releasing sigh after impatient sigh. Daniel imagined he'd be pacing the room if it weren't for the gaping hole in the back of his gown. The Marines had stripped

Daniel of his modesty a long time ago, but Cade hadn't had that sort of meat market initiation. He was as modest as any woman he'd ever known, which was ridiculous. He was a stunning male specimen. With his thick curly hair and lean build, he'd only become sexier with age, something Daniel envied.

"What time is it?"

"Ten minutes later than the last time you asked," he said after checking his watch. When Cade's worried expression turned into a scowl, Daniel stood and walked over to the bed, taking his face into his hands. "It's a simple procedure," he said and placed a calming kiss on Cade's lips. It was his turn to be Cade's soothing balm. "Same as last time. In and out."

Cade snorted. "Now you talk dirty?"

Unable to contain his laughter, Daniel shook his head and pressed his forehead against Cade's. "Fuck you," he whispered with a grin.

"Fuck you," Cade whispered back.

"I love you." Though they rarely said those words, they sprang from his heart with ease. "You'll be back in your workshop creating the world's next Ninja vacuum cleaner in no time."

Cade sighed. "First I have to fix the code in the anti-drone network we set up for Con and Car. Dani plans on having the first herd-monitoring fleet up before calving season. She thinks she can streamline cutting and monitoring the heavies."

"What do you think?" Daniel asked, glad to have stumbled upon the perfect distraction.

Cade shrugged. "It can't hurt. And if the weather turns bad, it could save a lot of time and manpower trudging in and out of the snow for checks. With the cameras, they can watch the calving field in the monitors and have more time to respond to problems or deal with the orphans."

"Ugh, the orphans."

Cade snickered. "I'll never forget the sound of your teeth chattering from clear across the field that winter."

"I'll never forget freezing my ass off trying to find that damn calf's stubborn mother and getting her to the calving shed," he said as he remembered his first calving season with the McLendons.

Cade laughed out loud, then pressed his hand against his stomach with a grimace.

"See? That's what you get for laughing at me." Daniel pointed his finger at him. "It wasn't funny. You saw the patches of frostbite on my ass."

"But it's still a very sexy ass," Cade said with another chuckle.

"Yeah right," he smirked. "Stupid cows. They're not supposed to walk off and leave their offspring lying in two feet of snow to fend for themselves."

"That's a cow for you," Cade said. "One of the most frustrating animals on the planet. At least now you know why I ran off and joined the Agency. I'm not cut out to be a rancher."

"Mr. Candelle, we're ready for you."

Cade sobered. Daniel immediately regretted the interruption. They'd found their comfortable rhythm for the first time since the diagnosis and losing it was almost painful.

He took Cade's hand as he lay back on the gurney, giving him a lingering kiss. "I'll be right here waiting for you," he whispered in his ear, quelling the sudden current of emotion rushing to the surface and gathering in his throat.

"Decide where else you want to go on our trip," Cade reminded him.

"I will."

Daniel watched as they wheeled him from the room, unable to move or breathe until a nurse took hold of his hand. "He'll be fine," she said and watched with him until the gurney disappeared behind a set of flapping double doors. "I'll walk you back out to the waiting room and someone will come get you when he's in recovery."

"Yeah." He followed her through the maze of hallways back to Gabby and Grey.

Waiting wasn't one of his strengths. He sat for a while, then paced for a while longer before settling into a seat in the most remote corner of the waiting room. Having foregone the omelet sandwich Grey procured from the cafeteria, his stomach churned, but the thought of eating was repulsive.

"How are you doing?" Gabby asked for the third time. He shrugged and shifted in his seat. Conversation was awkward. Every time he opened his mouth he was tempted to tell her about Jonah. He would've already spilled the beans, but figured a hospital wasn't the best place to drop that particular bomb. He would, though, once Cade was out of surgery and he could concentrate enough to keep himself together.

Gabby's purse rang, saving him from answering her as she reached inside and retrieved her phone. "It's Jonah!" she said with a gasp as she rose from her seat in a rush and swiped the screen to answer the call. "Jonah? Where are you? How are you?" Gabby glanced up at Grey, a surprised look in her eyes that quickly turned to confusion. "You're home? Right now? Is everything okay?"

Grey jumped from his seat and leaned in to listen to the call.

"We're at the hospital—or the outpatient center across the street— with Papa Daniel. No, honey, he's fine. It's..." She chewed on her thumbnail as she glanced at Grey. "It's Uncle Cade."

"Don't tell him over the phone," Daniel whispered with a shake of his head.

"He had another gallstone," she said with a nod. "Honey, we've tried calling you for weeks. Why haven't you returned our calls?"

Daniel looked away, unable to meet her gaze lest he reveal more than he should.

"Oh—okay. No. We're not sure how much longer we'll be."

"Let me talk to him," Grey insisted, reaching for the phone.

"You're dad wants to talk to you," Gabby said, holding up a finger to Grey. "Yes, Dad Grey. Matt and Mason took a ride up to the ridge to look for a few strays. Okay, honey. I'll be home soon. I love you! I can't wait to see you!"

Gabby handed the phone to Grey, her smile stretched from ear to ear as she leaned down and wrapped her arms around him. "He's home!"

Daniel hugged her back. "You can go home to see him if you want," he offered. "I'll be fine." He didn't need front row seats to the drama that would unfold once Jonah came clean about where he'd been all this time.

"No," she insisted, glancing at her watch, but he could see how much she wanted to. "It shouldn't be much longer.

"Are you sure? I don't mind," he insisted, hoping she was right. They were already more than an hour past the estimate Dr. Doom had given them. His thoughts wandered into the *what-if* minefield, but the commanding tone of Grey's voice diverted his attention.

"It better be a damn good explanation," Grey said into the phone, his stern voice carrying over the commotion in the waiting room.

Daniel looked up to see Grey standing by the window, his arm folded over his chest, a scowl on his face as he talked to Jonah. He didn't know which would be worse: facing another of Dr. Doom's firing squads, or facing Grey after putting Gabby through so much worry.

"Daniel." Gabby tapped his arm. He looked up to see Dr. Doom headed his way, dressed head to toe in dark blue scrubs.

His stomach knotted as he stood to meet him.

"Everything went well," the doctor said as he reached out and shook Daniel's hand. "Better than expected, actually." If breathing was something he had to think about doing, he would have passed out. "The gallstones are gone and the bile ducts are clear. The stints went in seamlessly."

"What about the tumor?" he asked. "Is it…"

"There's some intrusion into the gallbladder," Dr. Doom confirmed, "but it's not as bad as I imagined it would be. Not yet. He should have a few good months before we'll need to address pain management."

Beside him, Gabby released a long sigh of relief. Daniel didn't know whether to cry or shout for joy. It was good news. As good as it could get under the circumstances. "When can I see him?"

"A nurse will come get you as soon as he's settled in recovery," the Dr. said with a nod. "They'll give you the post-op paperwork and schedule a follow-up appointment before he's released."

"Thank you," he said and shook the doctor's hand one more time. "Thank you for everything."

As soon as the doctor walked away, Daniel braced his hands on his knees and took several deep breaths.

"Come sit down," Gabby urged. Grey hung up the phone and rushed over to him.

"I'm fine," he assured them, waiving away their offered support. "I'm relieved is all."

Thirty minutes later he was guided through the same set of hallways to another small room where Cade was resting on a gurney. The lights were dimmed, but there was no mistaking the lazy grin on his face when he saw Daniel walk in.

"There you are!" Cade said with a slow, drunken lilt, his voice a little scratchy. He lifted his arm and reached out over the bedrail for him.

"I wouldn't be anywhere else," Daniel said with a relieved sigh as he took his hand.

"You're so damn hot."

Heat bloomed beneath Daniel's collar and the nurse beside him giggled.

"I told you, didn't I?" Cade's glassy gaze drifted to the nurse. "He's the best damn lookin' yankee cowboy you'll ever meet."

"He sure is," the nurse said and gave Daniel a wink. "He's been singing your praises from the second he woke up," she whispered. "And a little bit of Glen Campbell, too."

The heat intensified and Daniel tugged at the collar of his shirt. "Sorry," he offered, unused to the unabashed flattery. He'd also heard Cade sing and could confirm, without a shadow of a doubt, Con and Car's singing talent did *not* come from the Candelle bloodline.

"Don't be," the nurse said with a flirty smile. "He's right."

"I'm thirsty." Cade released his hand and pressed his fingers against his throat. "And my throat hurts."

"I'll go get you some ice," the nurse offered and left the room.

"I want to drive a Batmobile," Cade blurted out of nowhere.

Daniel choked on a snort. "What?"

"Yyyyep," Cade said, popping the 'P' at the end. "For our trip. It'll be more fun than an RV."

"Ooo-kay." *How much of the good stuff did they give him?*

"Oh! That reminds me." Cade's eyes widened as he pointed a finger at Daniel. "I promised Dr. Doom if I didn't die I'd get him a green jacket. He needs a green jacket."

"We'll do that." Daniel chuckled.

"You know what else?"

"What?" Daniel laughed, almost afraid to ask.

Cade stared blankly at him for several long seconds, his brows furrowing into a deep 'V', his lips pressed together into a rigid line before he belted out, "I'm a rhinestone cowboy!"

What the hell?

"Yippee ki yay, mother fucker!"

"And now we're Bruce Willis," Daniel mumbled under his breath as he stood to go get the nurse. Something was wrong.

"Here you go," the nurse rounded the corner with a grin on her face and handed Daniel the cup of ice. "Remember, one piece at a time."

"Are you sure he's okay? You didn't overdose him?" Daniel asked. "He wasn't like this after the last time he had surgery. I've never seen him like this."

The nurse took the cup from his hand and held it to Cade's lips, suppressing another giggle. "He'll be fine," she assured him with a dismissive waive. "We've seen all kinds of crazy when people are coming out of anesthesia. Trust me, this is nothing. And as far as the difference, stress can be a real game changer. I'm sure he's had his fill of it lately."

Daniel took the cup from her hand, nodding skeptically as she left the room.

"Damn, that feels good," Cade said, sucking on the piece of ice.

Daniel fed half the chips to him, piece by piece, until he relaxed against the pillow, his eyelids closing on a sigh. When he opened them again, they were a little more focused, but not much.

"Come here," Cade whispered, motioning for him to come closer. Daniel leaned over until they were cheek to cheek and Cade pulled him down to lie on the mattress.

It took him several tries, and more flexibility than he possessed to get stretched out beside him, but once he did, Cade wrapped his arms around him and nuzzled the side of his neck.

"One of these days I'm going to marry you," Cade whispered into his ear.

Daniel stilled. The same deep-seated fear he'd always felt at the idea sparked through his body, making his skin tingle and itch. This time, however, it was tempered by a familiar guilt. He'd known. Deep down he'd always known that Cade wanted more. They'd played a screwed up version of don't ask-don't tell—Cade not asking so Daniel didn't have to tell him no. Dancing around his fears, compromising their love. And for what? He couldn't think of a single reason not to marry Cade.

Fuck-it, he heard Cade's voice in his head and grinned. Bit by bit, he released the last breath he'd taken and took another, finding Cade's hands and lacing their fingers together.

"Yes," Daniel said and closed his eyes. He imagined Cade standing before him in a suit, wearing his sexy cowboy hat, his lips turned up into that lazy, crooked smile of his.

"Yes, what?" Cade mumbled, the words slurred and broken.

Cade may not remember this moment after the drugs worked their way out of his system, but Daniel would. He'd push Cade to the courthouse in a wheelbarrow if he had to, but he had a feeling that wouldn't be necessary. The second he told Gabby, she and the rest of the family would plan a wedding they would never forget. He couldn't wait.

He brought Cade's hand to his mouth and kissed it, smiling against his palm as the words settled comfortably in his heart. "Yes, I'll marry you."

A True Love Story Never Ends

Want to know more about Daniel, Cade and the McLendons? See how it all began in

The McLendon Family Saga

The Heart of Falcon Ridge (Book 1)
A McLendon Christmas (Book 2)
Rock Star Cowboys (Book 3)
Rock Star Cowboys: The Honeymoon (Book 4)
The Hardest Goodbyes (Book 5)
Coming 2016
Return to Falcon Ridge (Book 6 – Jonah's Story)

Discover how Grant saved Natalie in their heart-stopping Romantic Thriller Series

Survivors' Justice

Surviving Redemption (Book 1)
One Defining Second (Book 2)

Thank You!

If you love Daniel and Cade's story as much as I do, please consider leaving a review. Be sure to sign up for my newsletter, or follow me on one of my many social media hang-outs listed below for behind-the-scenes updates on the entire McLendon family. Thank you for reading!

Stalker Links

Follow D.L. Roan for insider peeks of her upcoming books and get to know more about her cast of incredible, sexy characters.

www.dlroan.com
Facebook - DL Roan and Friends
Google+
Twitter
Facebook

eBooks available at the following eBook retailers:

Amazon
Apple
Barnes and Noble
Kobo
All Romance eBooks
Smashwords

Made in the USA
Monee, IL
23 March 2021